Prion

A Futuristic Fable of Parrots, Pandemics, and Promise-makers

LoraKim Joyner

Published by One Earth Conservation
Edition 1.1 February 2021
ISBN: 9780999207031
Library of Congress Control Number: 2020922140
First Edition First Printing
www.oneearthconservation.org
info@oneearthconservation.org
+1 (718) 776-7284

Prion: A Futuristic Fable of Parrots, Pandemics and Promise-makers. All proceeds from this book go to the 501 (c)(3) nonprofit organization, One Earth Conservation, which dedicates these funds to the people and parrots of the Americas.

Prion

Prions are abnormal, pathogenic transmissible agents that are able to induce abnormal folding of specific normal proteins called prion proteins that are found abundantly in the brain. The abnormal folding of the prion proteins leads to brain damage and the characteristic signs and symptoms of the disease, which includes rapid onset of dementia, trouble walking, and hallucinations. Prion diseases are usually rapidly progressive and always fatal.

To my spouse, Meredith, who makes all things possible, and more than a few probable.

and

To Rosa and Rebecca. Knowing of their deaths and others of their parrot-kind, may we humans find a way for all to fly free.

Contents

Prologue   1

South Island, New Zealand: Keas and Kiwis

        Chapter 1   7

        Chapter 2   13

        Chapter 3   21

        Chapter 4   31

        Chapter 5   39

        Chapter 6   49

        Chapter 7   59

South Australia, Australia: Cockatoos and Conferences

        Chapter 8   71

        Chapter 9   81

La Moskitia, Honduras: Scarlet Macaws and Miskitus

        Chapter 10   93

        Chapter 11   101

South Australia, Australia: Laboratories and Learnings

        Chapter 12   111

        Chapter 13   125

Kentucky, USA: Cages, Cockatoos, and Carolina Parakeets

Chapter 14   135

Chapter 15   147

South Australia, La Moskitia, Kentucky, South Island: Panorama of People and Parrots

Chapter 16   159

Chapter 17   173

Chapter 18   185

Chapter 19   197

Chapter 20   205

Chapter 21   213

Chapter 22   219

The Storm Room Miracle

Chapter 23   229

Going Home

Chapter 24   235

Epilogue   245

Context to Reality   255

Acknowledgements   259

Connecting   261

About the Author   263

If we will have the wisdom to survive,
to stand like slow-growing trees on a ruined place,
renewing, enriching it,
then a long time after we are dead
the lives our lives prepare will live there...

The abundance of this place,
the songs of its people and its birds,
will be health and wisdom and indwelling light.

This is no paradisal dream.
Its hardship is its possibility.

-Wendell Berry, excerpt from "A Vision"

Prologue
South Island, New Zealand: Sometime in the not too distant future

Aria looked down from Author's Pass and breathed out a frigid sigh. She wasn't going to make it before dark closed around her. The sun had disappeared over the highest peaks an hour ago, but she had thought she could make it to the road. She'd pushed herself to exhaustion but didn't seem to make much headway. Normally, it wouldn't be a problem to camp out alone in the mountains since there weren't any dangerous animals on South Island. But it felt like someone was following her, and that's why she had nearly run in the places she could. Every time she looked over her shoulder, though, all she saw was one or two keas, the large alpine parrots she always enjoyed. She recognized one with a band on her right leg who had been released from the Kea Foundation for Conservation, aka KFC. Aria worked there as a part-time veterinarian, using her mobile veterinary clinic for fieldwork and house calls. The other kea wasn't banded and was a stranger to her. Both followed her, but they often did that out of curiosity. The worst that they might do is run off with some of her food or camping equipment if she didn't keep an eye on them. She knew from her research with captive keas how smart they were. Right now, she wasn't thinking much about these smart, beautiful birds she had dedicated her life to. Though these parrots and the sparkling snow-capped mountains and meadows full of golden buttercups had been breathtaking, their beauty had not dispelled her growing sense of malevolence. She was in danger and couldn't escape what was coming for her.

She told herself not to be silly, that she'd watched too many zombie films. Or maybe it was that documentary about how decades earlier Covid-19 had blown through the world. She'd been just a kid, but the documentary had brought back a memory of shopping with her mother the night before the lockdown. The store was packed with long lines, anxious people panic buying food, guns, and ammunition. The crowds had started forming the day before the month-long lockdown. Holding her mother's hand, they were jostled roughly by two burly men trying to push in front of them to the gun counter.

"No way, Jose," her mother said and elbowed them back, not yielding any space.

Her mom had grown up in Honduras when it had the highest murder rate in the world, and she knew how to take care of herself. She also knew about guns, having married the descendent of a Maori sheep rancher, and she had been an accomplished hunter in her youth. They met when he arrived in her Miskitu indigenous village in Honduras to work in the community clinic.

Her mom placed her body between the glaring men and the gun counter and growled, "I'll take those two boxes of 20-gauge shells," the last two.

Quickly paying cash so they could leave, her mom nearly jerked Aria's arm out of its socket to leave the store. Looking over her shoulder, she saw hatred mixed with violent intent seething from the urban bullies following them to the parking lot.

"Hey, honey, did you get the ammo?" her father called as he walked up with his arms full of grocery bags to get them through the quarantine. One look at mom's face stopped him in his tracks. He looked behind her at the rapidly approaching men and dropped the bags, making the kumara potatoes spill with thudding sounds. Her dad yelled, "Hey, what's the problem here?"

The men stopped but didn't back away. They watched the family gather the kumara, leaving the few that rolled near the men's feet.

"Let them have them," her mom said as they jumped in the car, and she sped out of the parking lot, one hand on the wheel and the other on Aria's shoulder in a comforting squeeze. "Don't look back, Aria, just look forward." All the way home, though, it felt like they were still coming after them, stalking them to steal what was theirs. She had felt pursued throughout the coronavirus epidemic, and it took years for the fear to fade. And it had, until now.

She couldn't help looking over her shoulder. Where there had been two keas, there were now five. They don't usually congregate in the dark, unless... She had read stories about keas attacking sheep at night. Some keas ate sheep, alive. She told herself she must be near their nests or roost, and they were saying goodnight.

"Hey, guys, is there a problem? I don't want to bother you, but I have to spend the night here," Aria said aloud, as much to give herself company as to see the keas' response.

Her words were received as an invitation, and they walked towards her. Often choosing not to fly, she thought they looked as silly walking as penguins did. She pulled out her camp stove to boil water for supper. Now ten keas were only a few meters away, staring. Even that close, their brown plumage turned black under the moonless sky. Incoming clouds hid the stars. Her hands shook as she tried to light the stove. Finally, it ignited, and she saw 20 keas, some perched on her pack.

It was more keas than she'd ever seen flocking together this close to humans. "Hungry?" She pulled out a bag of pasta and kumara and threw two potatoes out of the radius of light for them, hoping the keas would sound the alarm if someone was following her. The flock hopped over to inspect the potatoes, some flapping their wings and exposing the bright burst of blood-red under their wings. "You sure are beautiful if spooky birds, big guy," she said to the one kea still atop her pack. He glared at her with intelligence and intention, then unzipped her main pouch with his beak and out poured chocolate and nuts. She shooed him away, but he nipped her hand, refusing to leave.

"Ouch, you little bugger." Keas often bit the tourists that fed them at ski resorts, and Aria felt it served them right for illegally feeding wildlife. But she was offended. She, like anyone who worked in parrot conservation, had rightfully earned her scars, a testament to the truth of her resume.

"You're the biggest kea I've ever seen. And you have one hell of a bite," she said as he rifled through her pack. She sucked the wound to keep the blood from dripping on her clothes or in her boiling water. When a few drops exploded on the pure-white snow, the other keas turned their heads, abandoned the potatoes, and waddled into the light. They had multiplied to 50 keas. "Glad you're here to protect me. And that I am so much bigger than you!"

As if challenged, the large kea hopped off her pack and walked to the boiling pot. More curious about than afraid of the intelligent and fearless keas, Aria watched the kea walk around the stove, and then go back to her pack and pull out her bandana. He walked back to the stove and shrilled twice, "Krrk, krrka." There was an explosion of red, this time of kea wing feathers as a cloud of parrots flew toward her. "Are you thirsty?" she said and backed away. So many birds were in the air that she couldn't see three keas grab the bandana in their beaks, drop it over the pot's handle that they then bit, and fly with the pot towards her. She was batting away the other keas, who were no match for her. She glanced up at movement overhead just as the keas dropped the pot of boiling water on her face. Aria fell screaming and grabbed fists of snow that she rubbed on her face. Her eyes tightly crumpled in pain. The keas dragged the stove to her and tilted the flames toward her parka. On fire, she thrashed and rolled to the cliff's edge. She hung on the blade of cliff over the abyss she knew was below. Grasping and grunting for a handhold, her kea pecked fists filled with brown and blood-red feathers as she fell. The dark flock swirled over her all the way down, calling, "Krri-ah, krri-ah," until her body landed broken. When the last of her clothes burned away, the big kea chortled to the flock, and with a rush of raised wings, her body had a new covering of feathered bodies. The keas' dexterous feet and sharp beaks were exquisitely evolved for the task beneath them.

Chapter 1
South Island, New Zealand

Maitita's old eyes had more wrinkles than a newly hatched kea chick. She could still see well enough to know that Turagg had landed nearby.

"Kruer," he clucked to tell her it was him. She shrilled back, irritated that he considered her so feeble as to not know that no one flew with the force he did, that no other kea was as large as he was. He hopped to her between the sun-bathed rock and the drift of snow near her ancient nest-home. She dug her beak into the snow and flicked some powder at him to let him know she didn't hold a grudge. As the oldest kea in the clan and on the island, she was both proud of her advanced age and the respect the younger ones showed her, but also shamed. She could no longer join the others in teaching the yearlings to forage. The last time she tried to fly over the mountains, she almost cleared the peak when coughing overtook her, and she had to turn back. Flying down to the coastal feeding patches was no easier. She could ride wind currents down, and on a sunny day she could take advantage of rising currents to return to her territory. But if clouds floated in to dress Mother Sun in grieving clothes, or if the clouds cried enough to wet her feathers, she didn't have the strength to flap fast enough to gain altitude. So, she spent most of her days near her nest. Alone often, she basked in the embrace of her sky parent, Mother Sun, warming her dull feathers, her mourning clothes. So great was her age that she had witnessed the great killing.

Thinking back so many Mother Sun turnings ago, a peep escaped her like some needy chick, she thought with shame. Turagg hopped closer and laid a coprosma berry beside her. Though young, he knew the kea traditions.

"Tell me, grandmother, where you hurt today. Is it your leg?" he asked as he lowered his head in submission, and perhaps to receive her soothing beak scratching. He saw how grandmother held her right leg out over the snow, and he knew it had been years since it could support her weight. He shoveled more snow under her leg to prop it up, and he pulled moss from a rock to cushion her leg.

"No, grandson, Mother Sun shines on me today. My leg is warmed and soothed by her, as is my heart with your visit."

"But why did you cry out? Tell me, grandmother."

"You would hear a story from me? Aren't you gathering the clan to guide them to the summer foraging grounds?"

"Not yet. We're still celebrating the summer's longest day."

"You young ones breed later than we did. It must be the warming windstorms that come so frequently now," she mused.

"Perhaps, grandmother. But I came not to talk to you of nests and eggs, but to seek your wisdom."

"There is nothing more important than nests and eggs. Our strength comes from our nest-homes, and our eggs are the future. I spend my last days here at my old nest-home, gathering memories to pass on to the clan. Every egg has inherent worth and beauty, and none is lost without grief. We have lost so many eggs and so many bright yearlings. But maybe this will all change, for I've heard great news. Is it true that your Junptra has given the flock three chicks that will fledge soon?"

"Yes, we have a nest-home full of strong and energetic chicks. I love them all so, but I don't know if love is enough."

"What troubles you?"

"No, you first, grandmother. The clan's business can wait. The flight will be made clearer if you tell of the great killing."

"You want to hear how we saved ourselves from being destroyed, don't you? We didn't save ourselves. It was the nonwinged ones who caused the avicide, and they are also the ones who saved us. I've told this story before the light of the waxing and waning night sky parent, Big Snowball, every winter's shortest-day for the last 20 years. Why do you wish to hear of darkness in this time of light?"

"Because times are changing, our people are changing, maybe like they did in olden times."

"Hah, you say olden, but if you go back even further, they were the golden times. Before the nonwinged ones set one stupid foot upon this land. Imagine trying to walk on feet that can't grip anything. Instead they had second feet where their wings should be, but these chest feet were as agile as their minds. Where once we roamed all over this island and played in the waves, riding on sea creatures' shells in the white surge, the nonwinged ones tore up our feeding and breeding grounds for their dead-tree homes and the strange hardfoot ones that accompanied them. This was before I was hatched. By the time I could fly, the only places for us were up in the highest reaches of the ridges because everything below had been turned into feeding grounds for their animals. They took what was ours, so it was theirs. Where there had never been hunger, there was hunger. And that's when the killing began.

In the long winter nights, in our gathering roosts, some of the old ones said it was our own fault this calamity came upon us, for we had started the killing first. But how could that be when the land was ours and our neighbors, even before the nonwinged ones tramped on the reaches of each clan? How could we refuse to feast upon the deceased hardfeet, those white fourleggeds who ate our grass and flowers, whose sweet bodies were abandoned by their own clans? First, we went to see why the hardfoot was so still, and then we wondered why the family had left them. We saw the nonwinged didn't value the hardfeet because they didn't move the passed ones or bury them, or set them in the trees so their spirits could soar upon every Mother Sun's rising. We poked and prodded at the white ones whose feathers were curly and tough and thick, trying to figure out what manner of being they were, and buried under thick curly feathers was skin like ours, and under this skin, food of such bounty! We ate them, and they sustained us, especially in the long winters far from our ancestral feeding grounds. Our numbers grew.

Then, sometimes, but not too often, a single kea, or a clan, would ride on the backs of these white ones, like they did once in the sea, enjoying the wild, erratic run. Others would poke and prod while they rode, nipping deeper and deeper until the living food was discovered, and a nibble could lead to consumption, and life came from life. I will not deny that some hardfeet died. But why, oh why, were the nonwingeds' hatred and vengeance so great? So immense was their fury to lose a few of their seemingly unworthy family that the snows ran red with our blood. For every hardfoot that died, thousands of our kin were shot, trapped, stolen, and their severed beaks hung from trees, their bodies heard no keening from the clan. We became lonely, scattered, and terrified. Until one day, a nonwinged turned from their ways and stayed her hand. She allowed the occasional sheep, she called them, to feed our hunger, and she convinced other nonwingeds to end the slaughter. That was many years ago, when I could fly over not just one but two mountain ridges in a day. Sometimes the killings persisted, but it was more an aberration than celebrated tradition for these keas. I think we may even call some nonwinged our friends. It's hard for me, because my entire clan was murdered, as was my first mate-to-be. We had not yet paired off and left our yearlings flock, but we knew in the depths of our hollow bones that our love was as clear and as full as the mountain air."

"Peep, peep." She tried to cover her chick's call by shifting her weight and raising her wings. "The red on our underwing feathers is a permanent sign of blood spilled and lives lost, the badge that all keas carry to remember that life is tragic and a yearling's frolic, blood and beauty."

Lifting his wings in ritual thanks for the sacred telling, her grandson opened his beak and gave the blood and beauty call, "Krri-ah," before bowing his head in silence. He sighed as Maitita reached out and preened his head, which he returned in kind.

She returned from her grief into the now and asked, "So what is troubling you, dear grandson?"

He stared off and said, "Thank you for the looking back. It helps us in this time of looking forward, because the killing has begun again."

Chapter 2
South Island, New Zealand

"Kee-a, kee-a," roared in Aria's ears as the kea's beaks dug into her. "Get 'em off, get 'em off," she moaned and rolled in the sheets that bunched around her neck.

"Kee-a, kee-a," thrummed against her heart that was pumping hard for what was supposed to be a lazy morning in bed to be followed by a New Year's Day trek into the mountains. She gasped as she woke to a huge kea staring at her, but it was the enlarged photograph that hung in her bedroom. Relief flooded her when she realized she was alive and she could see, and she was lying on her bed, not in a gravel valley at the base of a cliff. Wow, that was a nightmare for all time! "Kee-a! Kee-a!" She jumped before she remembered her new ring tone, a kea flight call. Digging in the sheets, she found the phone.

"Mom" spelled her screen, and the time, 7:30 a.m. Her heart started speeding again. Mom never called this early. She was usually out in the pastures on her daily rounds of checking on the sheep and keas. Something must have pulled her out of the routine to call at this hour. Aria hoped it wasn't Koro, her ailing grandfather who was healthy a year ago, but now was beset by rapid mental decline. Her fingers trembled, not in a nightmare but in awake time. She held her phone against her heart and hoped he was safe. Then she dialed. And dialed again. The phone didn't connect.

She thought her mother must be in some mountain valley pocket where the signal is weird, or maybe she has her hands full with whatever emergency might be happening. The dream had spooked her. Placing the phone on speaker mode, she climbed out of bed and dialed again. Looking at her phone, she didn't see the pillow she threw during her nightmare and her foot caught on it. The phone flew as she grabbed the bathroom counter, catching herself before she nose-dived into the toilet bowl rim. Her phone wasn't so lucky and did a perfect swoosh into the yellow-tinged bowl. She scrunched her nose and reached for the phone. A mumbled "Kee-a kee-a" vibrated the water. She snatched up the phone and ran it under the faucet, hoping her mother wouldn't give up after only a few rings. She told herself to get a new ringtone as she dropped the dripping phone on a towel and told her smart home system, "Answer phone in house speaker mode."

"Mom" she said as she turned and sat on the toilet bowl, her contact with water sending subconscious messages to her bladder that emptied now.

"Honey, are you okay, you sound out of breath? Are you out jogging? Is it raining there?"

"Nope, I'm just having one of those mornings. Didn't sleep well," she said.

"But are you okay? Has anything happened?"

Aria could hear the wind rushing over her mother's phone from whatever valley her mother was in. "Granddad Kora, is he okay?"

"Yes, he's fine, well, at least the same as yesterday. I've got an injured kea. That damn Isaac shot another one."

What happened? Is the bird bleeding? Where are you?" Aria rifled off questions as she looked for her pants.

"I'm about 30 minutes from home. The bird is weak. There's blood on her feathers. She's in my coat against my chest. I'm holding horse reins and the phone, so I can't talk long. Can you meet me here or at the KFC?"

Aria's fingers added the time for her mother's path to meet up with hers.

"I can get to the bird quicker if I meet you on the road. Ride home as quickly as you can without jostling the bird. Put her in a cardboard box and start driving to KFC. I'll start driving toward you."

"That's the plan then. *Tiksu*, Aria," said her mother, slipping into her native Miskitu language.

"Bye, Mom. Be careful. And thanks," but the line was already dead.

She grabbed her car keys and tripped on her boots. "I'm getting as bad as Granddad: falling, iffy bladder control, and talking to myself," she muttered as she picked up her boots and jogged down the hallway. She guessed she drank more draughts than she remembered last night during the New Year's Eve party at the pub next door. She was glad that at least she was still wearing a relatively clean shirt from yesterday and didn't have to look for one. As she passed the kitchen, she spied the coffee maker out of the corner of her eye. Set to read movement and sound in the house, it was already gurgling with the best smell in the world, next to a fluffed-up, feathered parrot belly. "Not today, Dr. Ropata!" she said. "You've got a bird to save."

She grabbed her jacket as she opened the door and pitter-pattered to the truck, her mobile vet clinic. "Ouch, ouch," she squeaked as gravel dug into her bare feet.

"I'm sorry I don't recognize that command," said her car. "Could you repeat?"

Throwing her boots in the passenger seat, she said, "Moana, start and plan the fastest route to my mother's."

The engine sparked to life, and the car said, "Please buckle up. I'll start moving as soon as you do."

"I'll drive today, thanks anyway."

"Okay, is there anything else I can do?"

"Yes, play ranchera music, and play it loud!"

She listened to the fast-paced music when she needed to gear up for action. It wasn't the music of her mother's Honduran home, but she liked anything from the Americas, where she'd done her residency in avian medicine. "No no no yo no me resignaré," blasted the speakers and she had to laugh. That was one of her mother's favorite songs from her own youth, "Dejami Vivir" (Let Me Live).

"That's right, let the parrots live, and I won't give up, won't give up," she sang along as she pulled onto the expressway to her parents' ranch north of Springfield. But Kea conservation was hard. It was at a crossroads, and it wasn't looking good. The birds were protected, but continual habitat destruction to make room for the livestock industry had intensified in the last decades, causing more conflict because the hungry keas were scavenging in human areas and, like in every other century, pestering the sheep, and sometimes feasting on them. But what had tipped the scale was climate change.

"Moana, roll down the windows. It's going to be a hot one

today."

As the windows sank down, Moana said, "I can turn on the AC if you like."

"No, we better not, mitigating climate change and all that."

"As you wish," said Moana.

"I love you, too, Moana." She smiled, feeling like she was in a vintage movie.

The hot wind in her face felt good, but the aroma of cattle feedlots was putrid. She couldn't understand why people still ate meat. She rolled her eyes and shook her head, glad that her mother had almost completely knocked meat out of her diet. She ranched sheep only in select areas of the farm, mostly as a picturesque backdrop for their ecolodge, Kowhai Ranch.

"Do you want to go to one of your favorite vegan restaurants?"

"No, let's just get to Mom's. We can worry about eating later. Sing along with me." "Dejame vivir!" sang out the trio, harmonizing along Highway 78. Several songs later she said, "Moana, call Mom and see where she is. And turn off the music."

"Hey *mija*, I'm at the Crosby ranch. Where are you?"

"I'm 10 minutes away. How's the kea doing?"

"She's standing fluffed up in her box. She must be pretty badly hurt if she isn't trying to figure out how to rip up the box, let alone get out."

"Did you see her get shot?"

"No, I was on the north side of our ranch when I heard a shot echo through the valley, followed by either a motorcycle or ATV. I rode Aras at full speed to see what was up. By the time we got there, whoever shot the kea was long gone. I suspect it was Isaac. His ATV tracks were in the pasture near his ranch. There was a dead ewe in the pasture, one of Isaac's. A Turcana, and by the look of her, she'd been dead awhile."

"Where did you find the kea?"

"That's the odd thing. And by the way, the kea is Juniper," said her mother.

"But Juniper has chicks in the nest!"

"Making Isaac doubly in trouble. By hurting her, he may have doomed the entire brood."

Aria said, "Thank goodness males are the primary food gatherers, so they might be okay. And the chicks were ready to fledge, which may be why Juniper was far from home. Is that what was odd about Juniper being near the dead ewe?"

"Juniper wasn't near the sheep. I was looking all around when Aras' ears shot up, spooked, and that horse doesn't scare easily. But something rattled him. He was staring at a nearby Kowhai tree, where about 20 keas were dark and quiet, including the injured one, and more were flying in. I don't know how she got up in the tree because she was unconscious. The keas were cradling her with their beaks and feet so she wouldn't fall. They didn't fly away when I rode up, but they almost never do. I saw blood near the sheep where Juniper was shot, and under the tree where they must have carried her. I didn't know how I was going to get her down. As I rode under the tree, I heard the keas softly keening that 'Kee-na, kee-na' call they sometimes use when stationary. I recognized a few of them from the ranch roost, and I think they knew who I was. Then one called, 'Krrk, Krrk,' and they began slowly lowering Juniper branch by branch to me. They watched me wrap her in my coat. Some followed me to the ranch, and they might still be there for all I know."

"You've got to be kidding me! I swear those birds are

smarter every year. And of course, they recognize you, and looks like they trust you as well. You've been protecting them even longer than Grandma Maggie did. She did so much of the groundwork by asking her neighbors to quit shooting them and helping pass the law that made it illegal to harm them, even if they pestered or killed sheep. But you have spent decades day in and day out, side by side with the keas. Hey, I see your car up ahead. Bye!"

Two generations of women simultaneously swerved their trucks onto opposite shoulders and braked, as if performing a choreographed dance. They ran towards each other, one with a small box and one with a med kit. Donika held her breath as her daughter slowly opened the box.

Aria said, "I can't see where she's shot. She's got the blanket bunched in her foot against her left side. Where did you see the blood?"

"On her left side."

"Huh, it's like she's putting pressure on her wound," Aria whispered as she examined Juniper. "Well, she isn't bleeding now, that I can see, at least externally, and her breathing is normal. I think she'll be okay until I can get her to the clinic at KFC. I don't want to handle her now. A ride in the oxygenated incubator will get her ready for handling."

"Should I come with you in case you need an extra set of hands? She's one of the old one's granddaughters. I want to make sure she's okay."

"Wow, you know your flock well, Mom. Nah, I've got this. I know you've got a busy day prepping for your annual New Year's Kea Party tonight. I'll give a call once I treat her. What are you going to do about Isaac?"

"Don't your worry about that. I can handle him. You take care of Juniper."

"Okay. Bye. Talk to you later and if Juniper is okay, I'll see you at the party tonight."

Aria approached the open door of her car. "Moana, start the car and drive me to KFC." She wanted her hands free to examine Juniper, and treat her if needed before she arrived. She was worried about the bird, and ever more so about what her mother would do to Isaac.

Chapter 3
South Island, New Zealand

Donika spun into Isaac's ranch road, her angry speed trailing dust behind her. It had been a dry December, drier and hotter than any she remembered. She thought if the loss of biodiversity and climate change didn't kill them, then idiots like Isaac would. She had never seen him act as anything less than a *cabron* since they first met. Kaleb had told her he had a troubled twin brother, but she wasn't prepared for the almost mocking glare Isaac gave her when many years ago she stepped for the first time into the old ranch house where Maggie and Callum Roberts lived, and where Callum had been born. Their sheep ranch had been Maori land for hundreds of years, and it was where Kaleb had proudly brought his new and visibly pregnant spouse. Isaac shook her hand and held onto it a little too long while he asked, "So you stole my brother away. I hope your tamales are as good as he told us they are." With one fell stroke, he had tried to put her in her place as an outsider who was there to cook. Instead, she gripped harder so he would feel the calluses on her hand. She wouldn't let him spoil this wonderful homecoming for Kaleb who had been gone from New Zealand for three years. The last month they had been in quarantine before they could travel freely around New Zealand.

She said, "Where I come from, we don't cook tamales. The men cook while the women work the fields," which she knew wasn't true. The women did everything, cooked, cleaned, raised the children, farmed, and fished. She had learned to cook tamales when studying in the Americas, and hence was the only and therefore the best tamale chef in her village, Kaskatara. She couldn't do much else in the kitchen, but her community was proud of her ability as a hunter. She was one of the few women hunters the village ever had, and one of the best. This made her willful against traditional ways, but she had also gained respect for hard work, and anyone who could supply meat was treasured.

But no one had ever adored her as much as Kaleb had. The young New Zealand doctor had traveled from this far-off island country to staff the missionary clinic on the Coco River, which divided the pine savannah of two countries, Honduras and Nicaragua. Donika was a nurse at the clinic, one of the few in her area to leave the Miskitu region of Honduras to attend university in Tegucigalpa. She smiled inwardly remembering her dear Kaleb, now more than 20 years gone, lost during the Corona Flu Years. The smiled was replaced by a tight frown that gathered the folds of her face into a single thought. She blamed Isaac for both Kaleb's and Maggie's deaths. Kaleb may have contracted the virus from his work at the Christchurch hospital. But not Maggie, who was at risk from the virus because breast cancer chemotherapy had immunocompromised her. Despite that, Isaac broke quarantine, coming and going during her treatment. The fallout from the tragic deaths for Donika, other than long years of mourning for Maggie with Callum, and raising Aria without Kaleb, was that Isaac moved out of the family home and bought the neighboring farm. The farm where she had just arrived.

"*Dios mio*," she said as her car's swirling dust caught up to her on the porch. She stepped over a weathered saddle and kicked beer cans away. Pounding on the paint-chipped blue door brought no response. She tried again, yelling, "Isaac! It's Donika. I know you're in there." She tried the door. Locked. Probably he was still out on the land. She walked to the barn on what was barely a path through the carnage of a lost man's domestic ways and saw the ATV was gone.

This stoked her inner anger until it collapsed into fear that he was out killing more keas. He knew where they fed and roosted. He had grown up on Kowhai Ranch, the center of all things kea since the early 1970s. Then a young Maggie had led the charge to pass the laws that partially protected the keas, ending the killing spree of an estimated 150,000 keas. In 1986, she was instrumental in bringing about the Wildlife Act that prohibited ranchers from killing keas, even if they harassed or killed their sheep. But on Kowhai Ranch, keas hadn't been shot for a decade before when Maggie convinced Callum to let the birds be. Since then, Kowhai had been a sanctuary where the authorities could bring injured keas for release, as well as relocate some of the problematic keas that had gone "rogue." Maybe that's what Isaac had done; he'd finally gone rogue and let loose his personal demons on an innocent bird.

She vowed she wouldn't let that happen again as she started her truck. She enjoyed the physicality of her old "dumb truck" that Aria teased her about. Smart vehicles weren't as dependable on windy sheep roads and trails, and nothing could compare to her horse of many years, Aras. She loved that name, for it meant horse in Miskitu and always reminded her of home. Like Aras, she knew the valleys, hills, and ridges of her adopted home as well as she had known the tropical forests of her birthplace. With truck or horse, or on foot, she had no doubt that she could find Isaac. He never left the back roads for very long, but she was surprised he was still out so late.

Corral after corral along the way was empty with no sign of Isaac. Driving up a dry track that ran parallel to her ranch, she reached the spot opposite where she'd found the injured kea. "Kee-a" sounded as she looked up. Several keas were swirling in the updrafts over the western ridge. With no better idea, she headed in that direction. Keas were curious and might be tracking Isaac while keeping their distance from him and his guns.

Like crows, keas' wild language had "words," in this case words that distinguished "human" from "human with gun." She wondered if that was what they were saying now, or maybe, "Here comes the dark face one from the good human home," as her truck crested a hillock into the border valley of Isaac's ranch.

About 100 keas in the kowhai trees bordering the canal didn't startle when she climbed out of the truck. It's as Aria recently said, she had been caring for and releasing keas for decades, and many of them knew her, but not that whole tree full. Scientists had proven that keas could communicate recognition of specific faces, like crows, to other flock members, and maybe that was what was going on here. Donika wondered why so many were there when there was no food nearby.

That's when she saw Isaac sprawled next to his overturned ATV. She rushed to him, concern mixing with irritation. Maybe he was no threat to the keas now, but it was going to cost her the rest of the day to tend to the mess he'd gotten himself into. As she approached, she could see his face was slack, cut, and bleeding. Through the fog of years, he looked like the ghost of Kaleb come to haunt her. Kaleb had a soft spot for his twin brother, even though he barely tolerated him at times. "Kaleb, for you, I'll see this through," she whispered.

As she knelt down to check for injuries and Isaac's breathing, motion made her look up. Some of the keas had flown to a close kowhai tree and were looking down at her, staring, cocking their heads, chortling and clacking.

"I have no idea what you're saying, but let me apologize on behalf of all humans, and for this one in particular. I know your kind are disappearing, hell, so are mine, but I promise you're safe here. I'll make sure Isaac never bothers you again. Also, Aria said Juniper is going to live."

At that, the largest kea dropped from the tree and swooped toward her. She ducked, but didn't need to. The bird alighted on her hat briefly before flying off with it to the tree. The kea then raised his wings, displaying his under-wing red feathers, and called, "Krri-ah, krr-iah." In a call and response, the others cried," Krri-ah-ah, krri-ah-ah," and raised their wings. The large male flew off with the hat, struggling to gain altitude with the extra weight until another kea took a corner of the hat and they rose. A large wing feather fluttered to Donika's feet. She picked it up as the entire flock climbed the sky and disappeared, leaving her alone and open mouthed. She didn't know what she'd seen, but it was an honor.

A moan from Isaac drew her back. "Isaac? Isaac, wake up. Are you okay?" She knelt next to him, weaving the feather into her long braid.

"Where do you hurt?"

"Everywhere!" His ragged breath poured a fog of sour alcohol over her.

"Can you move your legs or arms?"

In answer he rolled onto this back and flipped her off with both hands. The same old Isaac, defiant in the face of something more serious than he could imagine.

"You look terrible. Can you walk? I can get you to the hospital."

"Just give me an arm up and help me right my ATV."

"You idiot, your neck might be broken. And your ATV looks as banged up as you."

He concentrated on moving his right leg, but when he moved his left one, he shrieked and sat up. "My neck's okay, but my leg isn't."

"Just sit there. Let me prepare the way." She opened her truck's passenger door, cleaned debris off the passenger seat, and then went to the ATV to get his personal items. She started humming an old tune from *Godspell*, one of Kaleb's favorites. Despite the seriousness of the moment and her anger, she sang, "Prepare ye the way..." She yanked the keys out of the ignition and pocketed them.

Turning back to Isaac, she found him flat out on the ground again. "Let me see your eyes," she said. Isaac opened them with a squint of pain narrowing their aperture. She could see no abnormal pupil size or eye movement, tested by flipping him off in return, moving her hand from right to left. "Well you look okay, but maybe we should call an ambulance."

"Are you kidding? It'll take hours to get one here from Christchurch and cost me the farm. I've got no pain in my neck or back, and my eyes are okay, so I'm not concussed. It hurts to breathe, but that's my ribs. There's blood on my leg, but the bleeding isn't arterial and has mostly stopped. Also, no bone poking out. Get me in the truck, and we'll take it from there."

She agreed only because he'd gone to medical school with Kaleb, but he hadn't finished. Kaleb had told her that was when things went wrong for Isaac. She knelt, and he put an arm around her and used the other to push for the momentum to help pull him upright.

She said, "On three. One, two, three!"

With a deep grunt from both and with graceless technique, Isaac was standing on one foot and leaning on Donika. Hopping to the side of the truck, he let her maneuver him onto the seat, grimacing as he tried to lift his leg into the truck.

"Swing my leg in."

"It's going to hurt."

"I know. Let's get it done."

Two sharp gasps later, Isaac was settled in, buckled up, and they were on the way. He leaned his head back and closed his eyes.

"Talk to me. Keep me awake to make sure I'm not bleeding internally."

"What do I do if you lose consciousness? Drive faster?"

"Yeah and start praying. In fact, you can start now if you'd like."

Isaac, always the comic, now let sincerity break through the alcohol, perhaps motivated by pain, or something else. She couldn't read him.

"Tell me what happened. And don't think because you're injured that you aren't in a lot of trouble for shooting the kea.

27

You could go to jail for that. Frankly, I'd like to see that happen."

"How do you know it was me? Can't prove a thing."

"I heard a shot and went to see what happened, and there was a wounded kea and fresh ATV tracks leading to your ranch. That's how."

"Whether I did or didn't shoot the kea, they deserve it. I've been losing too many sheep in the higher pastures."

"Hah, if you've lost any sheep, it's not their fault, but yours. That ewe had been dead a while. You need to keep better track of your sheep."

"I'm starting to regret asking you to talk to me."

"You talk then. What happened? Got drunk and wiped out?"

"I'm not drunk, but what happened feels like a nightmare. I was coming down the track when shadows flitted in front on me. Then suddenly a black cloud of keas swooped at me. Some of them landed on my head and on the back of the ATV, the same way they ride a sheep they're pecking at. The next thing I knew, I lost control and then blackness. Except–"

"Except what?"

"In that blackness, I was covered in keas that were tearing at my clothes, trying to feed on my skin, just like they dig at wool to get to a sheep's back fat." By way of explaining the story, he pulled at his clothes, which were torn and cut in ways that wouldn't be explained by a rolled ATV. Silence grabbed them both. Only the truck engine anchored their minds in a reality they both understood.

Finally, Donika said, "Hah, that's an alcohol and trauma hallucination. We both know that keas never attack humans." But even as she said it, she remembered stories around the campfires of hikers and hunters who had gone missing in the wilder alpine stretches. Perhaps not killed by keas, but rumors were that those foolish enough to die in the backcountry served themselves up as an accidental buffet for keas. She recalled the injured kea being cared for in the tree by other keas, and the weird, almost ritualistic display by the keas at the accident. Something had shifted in the Kowhai flock. She would study the live cams at each kea nest site to see what happened.

"Whatever happened, the shot kea lay right where you're sitting now."

Isaac scooted over, saw his fresh blood stains mixed with muddy smudges.

"I found her while I was riding the back pastures. I drove her to Aria who's working on her now at the KFC. It looks like the kea will survive, and so will you."

Donika was talking to an empty seat. Isaac had slipped into sleep, dreaming of blood and feathers raining from the sky and blanketing the earth.

LORAKIM JOYNER

Chapter 4
South Island, New Zealand

Turagg arrived winded at nest-home. The hat of Good-helper proved a chore to bring up the slopes, where his children waited to be fed. He wondered how he was going to feed their three fledglings without Junptra, the kea the nonwingeds called Juniper. The nonwingeds made odd sounds, but he was able to understand some of it and guessed at the rest. When his beloved was lowered into the hands of Good-helper, he heard her say Juniper several times, wiping rain from her face. The sky was clear, so he understood that the rain came from Good-helper, whose face was tight and whose not-beak showed displeasure. All keas were taught to read nonwingeds' faces so they knew when there was danger, and when a morsel of food might be offered (or stolen).

He dropped Good-helper's hat and lowered his head, but Junptra wasn't there to offer a comforting beak and ease his pain. He thought her injury was his fault, that he shouldn't have let her leave the home-nest. But the chicks had proven they could fly short distances. It was a long four months of child rearing, and Junptra was ready to stretch her wings. But now he needed her help to feed the family. Three chicks! In stories the grandmother told, heroes had three children all at once, but he'd thought they were made up to encourage youngsters to be the best they could be. Eat well and your children will live!

Junptra was a hero to him. She had spent all that time down in the dark underground nest, first with quiet eggs, then with helpless peeping chicks smooth-skinned as nonwingeds, and finally with rambunctious nestlings curious about everything and who seemed to never tire of play. Just last night he and Junptra were in a preen pile with the three, telling one story after another, waiting, waiting for them to fall asleep. They eventually did, and the weary parents shared moments of preening before he left to keep watch from the tree shading the entry to their deep-nest. He slept well, one part of his brain always drowsily awake, like all his feathered kind, watching the fire points chased by the night sky parent, Big Snowball. Then came Mother Sun, the giving sky parent who chased the sky points and Big Snowball away, and the morning that he wished he could take back.

"Kuer, kuer," cried his first hatch who poked her head out of the cavity. He lifted his head and called back, "Kuer. Crnac, first-one, come here and bring your brother and sister."

He needn't have given any instructions because already the non-ceasing tussling had begun among his three chicks. They had grown so fast, he could now call them fledglings. It wouldn't be much longer before they'd be on their own, maybe even sooner, with the mountain winds changing. He was tackled and covered by squirming and surprisingly heavy bodies. It wasn't much of a wrestle time, because almost immediately they bounced off him, lowered their bodies and heads, puffed up with wings out, and asked for breakfast. But Crnac stood upright, feathers sleek against her body, calling "Turagg, where's Mama

Junptra?"

The food from Turagg's crop that had been rising to feed the brood caught in his throat. He swallowed, and went to the nest rock, flapping a bit to not just reach the top, but so they could see the red feathers under his wing. His children stilled at his ritual display. This wasn't their usual breakfast stories. This was a blood and beauty story, their first.

"We flew towards the waking Mother Sun, to a place of good and plentiful food. Your mother's flight was perfect and strong, surely the most beautiful one to gather in the trees over the nonwinged's hardfoot track, where they go with their smaller white fourlegged companions. She was greeted warmly by friends she hadn't seen since your egg time, and there was a chortling of nest news. The whole clan had heard that she was mother to three chicks, that's you, Crnac, Trraw, and Kgraw, and they encouraged her to be first to feed, and she was. But as she landed, a nonwinged, hidden in the bush, let loose his kill-stick that knocked your mother to her side."

"Kee-na," his children's keening began.

"Be brave, young ones, the attack didn't kill her, but she was sorely injured. We had flown at the kill-stick's loud rain-hammer, but didn't go far, ready to do something, needing to do something. We knew this baldskin, this nonwinged, for he was Rockboy. Anger rose in me." The chick's keening now began in earnest, first in shock that their mother was hurt, and now to hear Papa use a naughty word instead of saying the more polite nonwinged, "Kee-naaaa–"

"I knew him as the one who hurt grandmother all those years ago by throwing a rock, and the blood feather time rose in me. Just as I started to fall from the perch to fly at him, he looked at the far hills, for he heard what we did, the thunder steps of a large hardfoot coming our way. Rockboy turned and walked into the bush, and then we heard the nonwinged fourroundfeet grumble, and we knew that he would leave us. At that sound I flew down to Junptra who had red on feathers where there should have been none. She was breathing. I laid my beak against hers, but she didn't wake.

"Krrk, Krrka," I called, and the flock flew to us. We took hold of her and flew her into the tree, where she would be safe from any ground hunters. My hope was she would wake and fly to where she'd be safe, maybe all the way home.

"Prrwak, prrwak," called Bruka, one among others that had followed close behind Turagg, and now gathered near the nest-perch for the telling. "You know that nowhere is safe!"

"Will you let me finish the telling? To my children!"

Bruka bowed his head, and Turagg continued.

"Then came Good-helper with her large hardfoot friend. She had helped injured keas before. We gave Junptra to her, so she would care for your mother until she could return to us. We lowered her to Good-helper, who took her in her arms and left with her hardfoot friend. Some of us flew off with her to make sure Good-helper was going to take Junptra to safety, while the rest of us held council about what we should do.

"Krwap!" sounded Bruka to those who were crowding around branches and rock piles. Nearly the entire clan was there except for the females with chicks in their nests. The word had traveled, causing anger mixed with fear for what the future held for their children. "You know we must fight back. For far too long these baldskins and their hardfoot family have taken our lands and our lives! Tell them now of our blood and beauty!"

Turagg said, "We flew after the Rockboy in blood-feather formation. Once we saw him, we bound our hearts to overtake him. We flew at his face, screaming our anger so he would at last listen. Instead he kept going and we swooped, showing him our red, our power, and yet we seemed powerless. Still we kept on in our flock-madness until the fourroundfeet, with a mind of its own, swerved from the hardfoot track and flipped over, spitting out Rockboy.

"We perched in a nearby tree to study what we would do next. Rockboy lay as Junptra had a short time earlier. 'Kring, krri-ah,' escaped me, my anger flying with sorrow when I saw the land turn the blood-red of Mother Sun low in the sky. I raised my wings, blood and beauty, and flew to him with no intent, but knowing deep pain and deep hunger. He would be dangerous if he woke. I pulled at his clothes. His body trunk moved, so he was alive, but not aware, as was Junptra. I pulled harder and harder, still no response. A piece of his skin-cover hung in my beak. It had torn like wool does from a hardfoot. I turned, and the eyes of my flock mates awoke the most dizzying love I've ever felt, even more than when I courted your mother. I raised my wings to them and the world. I didn't know what this love meant or what I could do with it, as it was also mixed with hate. I turned back to my tearing madness, and the flock joined me in a shared shredding that is the nature of our kind.

"Suddenly, my blood thirst was replaced with a clearness and a desire for newness, like a mountain spring giving birth. I saw a river of blood flowing into the future, and the world was like a winter sky after a white-covering fell. I saw so many possibilities. I had choices. We all have choices. I saw we could become something different, something better, something more powerful. My attention turned to Rockboy and my dear flock.

"Though my blood thirst had drained, I could see in your eyes, you there, Bruka, and you there, Chiznrk, that the thirst in you had not reached its peak. I don't know what would have happened if we hadn't heard a large fourroundleg rumble coming toward us. We flew to the tree to watch.

"Good-helper had come to help Rockboy, as she had Junptra earlier. She looked up at us, and she saw me and I saw her, as if clearly for the first time. She began to speak, and I saw her as if she had feathers and was one of us. I don't exactly know what she said, but I felt it was a blood-feather pact. I flew down and traded her extra head-skin for one of my feathers.

"Kwing, kwing," I called, and we flew home, taking sorrow and anger with us, but also something more. We took promises and choices, leaving Good-helper to do her work, for now we too have work to do."

He looked out at the nearly 150 gathered, and then at his three. His first order of business was to give life and feed, feed and give life, but he had no food left in him. Trinnie came forward, an old uncle with no nest of his own, and fed Turagg's three.

"What is our work?" asked Chinzz, an up-and-coming young male, as Trinnie stepped back into the crowd. A sharp chortling broke out and many voices said, "Yes, yes, what do we do now?" and feet raised in unity.

"I brought this head-skin from Good-helper to help us decide," Turagg said as he retrieved the head-skin from the nest-tree. The chicks were sleepy after eating, but the head-skin piqued their curiosity. It was all Crnac could do to not rush forward and touch her beak to the strange object.

Turagg said, "She made a promise to us, and me to her. I have ideas, but I would hear from you first."

"We should flee this area, move higher up to our mountain summer homes," said Uncle Trinnie. "We were going as soon as the last chicks fledged anyway. Let's be safe. Let's stay alive." Some clacked their beaks at this.

"This is old history. We'd be berry-less for the season," said Bruka, pacing as he spoke. "We have all listened to grandmother's story when our ancestors tried that before. Already our numbers keep dropping and our chicks are fewer. We should fly in groups as we did today, 100 strong, and attack the baldskins. See what we accomplished today? We can kill them." He added with a whisper, "We can eat them."

Many beaks clattered loudly, for Junptra had been popular and their blood had not yet stilled. They hungered for Rockboy revenge, as the story would be called for generations.

"But it's prohibited to kill," protested Tapwrok, a sister of Turagg. "If we attack, they'll come after us, like in the old story when there were hundreds of rockboys. Today there may be only one Rockboy, but there are untold numbers of nonwingeds who will come after us. Do we want that?"

"Yet, if we do nothing," said Chinzz, "they and their hardfeet will continue destroying the land. We have so little feeding territory and fewer trees because of fiercer storms and fires set by the striking anger bolts that come from Mother Sun.

"It isn't Mother Sun who sets most of the rockboys' fires, but the baldskins," Bruka claimed. "They need to go!"

Wings raised, and red flashed from all sides.

"But what of those nonwingeds who've given us sanctuary, such as Good-helper?" Tapwrok raised her voice and turned to

37

the flock. "She shares her land with us, cares for us, and sets out food when times are hard for us. Her eye-box watches over us to see that we are well." At that, each kea head twisted to the eye-box on a post that was the far eyes of Good-helper and her team. This slowed the rhythm of the wing raising, but not completely.

Turagg's deep voice said, "We have no consensus," and his three chicks fluffed with pride. "I may have lost my mate to one nonwinged's cruelty, and I have held baldskin covering in my beak. I knew anger and hunger together, a dangerous mix that turns heroes into foes. I wanted to dig deeper to ease my pain, but instead of tearing baldskin apart, I wanted to have other choices. We are more powerful than we know. We can raise three chicks! I see a time when every nest-home will have two and three chicks, and we will be plenty. I made a promise to Good-helper today, and she promised me. We are safe here for now while we make new plans to take back what is ours."

Finishing, unsure how his words would be heard, he picked up the head-skin and walked over to the eye-box and hung it over the lens, choosing not to tear it apart or ignore it, but to use it as a tool. "Now is the time to claim what they have stolen and make it ours. We shall fight in our kea way!"

Feathers sleeked even tighter to their bodies, and their necks stretched toward the now blind eye-box. They had never used a nonwinged beak-object with such purpose and promise for themselves, only for the nonwingeds who manipulated them to do chores with food.

"Krri-ah, krri-ah. We will blind the baldskins with our beak and claws," cried Bruka. "Blood and beauty flock mates!" He raised his wings, and they all did the same. He cried again, "Krri-ah-ah," and they flew wing-to-wing to fulfill the New Promise.

Chapter 5
South Island, New Zealand

After Donika drove Isaac to the emergency room of Christchurch Hospital, she stayed in town to run a few errands. The Kea Foundation for Conservation's New Year Gala was that night at her house, and she had too much to do to sit around an emergency room with Isaac. Despite herself, she was worried about him. She wanted him to quit killing keas, but she didn't want him dead. She checked her watch and decided she had enough time to drop by the KFC before returning to the ranch. Her car might not be smart, but her phone was. "*Guara*, call Aria."

"Kee-a, Kee-a," rang Aria's phone, interrupting her thoughts of how much she enjoyed working with the keas, despite her nightmare. Aria lifted Juniper from her recovery incubator into her hospital cage. "Hey, Mom. Please tell me you didn't rough up Isaac."

"I didn't have to. The keas beat me to it. He had an accident on his ATV. I just dropped him off at the hospital."

"The keas did what? Is he okay?"

"He could talk and mostly walk when I left him, so I think he'll be all right. Can I visit Juniper? I'm in town."

"She's awake from the surgery, and I just moved her from

the incubator. They've never made a kea-proof incubator. She was looking pretty perky, despite being shot and having surgery."

"Oh, that's good to hear. I'll be there in five minutes."

Juniper was fluffed, not her usual sleek self, but her eyes tracked Aria as she moved about the room preparing a meal for her.

"So, Juniper, the bad news is you were shot, and I had to surgically remove two pellets. The good news is it was nontoxic shot and no bones were broken. The bad news is that I don't think you'll fly for a while. You'll have to stay in the hospital for at least tonight before you go to Kowhai Ranch's Rescue Center. The good news is the hospital food is excellent. We've got berries, concentrate parrot kibble, flowers, and seeds. Here you go!"

Nikau walked in and looked over Aria's shoulder. "How's Juniper doing? I mean Junptra. I analyzed a bunch of tapes of this flock and at their nest site. When Junptra comes into contact with her chicks or with her mate, they call out Junptra, not Juniper."

"Good to know. Nobody likes being called by the wrong name, eh, Junptra?"

At that, Junptra made a peeping sound, reverting to chick behavior, which parrots often do when sick or injured.

"Of course, we can't make sounds like keas can. And without the computer analysis, I'm not sure I could ever hear all the different names they have for each other, let alone all their words," Nikau finished softly, in fear he had over-explained. "But I think we owe it to them to listen as closely as we can to honor their language and dialects."

"Spoken like a true postdoc and director of our Parrot

Communication and Intelligence Studies. But was it just a fluke that we called her Juniper that's so close to the name her parents gave her?"

"I wonder if when you were working with her when she was a chick, they heard you call her that and named her based on what they heard," he said.

"You mean they picked my name for her? That's not such a great thing if humans are taking over the kea language, especially with the name of a tree that isn't native."

"I wouldn't worry about that. We, or at least our computers, can make out over 500 kea words, and none are even close to human words."

"But they understand us, right?" Aria said.

"Yes, it's been shown that several species of parrots aren't just mimicking human speech, but they use it in context and even make up new phrases to get their meaning across. Many of them use syntax, not only in a human language, but in their own."

Junptra was listening closely while nibbling the fresh berries.

"She always seems to know what I'm saying. We better not say anything we'll regret."

"I don't do that. I mean what I say. Especially with you last night at the pub."

"At the pub?" Aria quickly scanned her memory and she came up with nothing that approximated a close conversation with Nikau, though her tummy did flips as he stepped toward her. He had started work only a few months ago, and it was true she liked him.

"You don't remember, do you? It was a bit fuzzy to me, too, until I found this napkin in my pocket," he said and handed it to her.

She read on one side, "We promise our lives and our love ..." Aria tried to look blank, despite conflicting emotions. She turned the napkin over. "... to protect keas and other parrots until death. None are free until all are free!"

"I remember. We were talking about the movement, Unconditional Solidarity, US, where members vow which wildlife to protect. I don't regret making that vow."

"Neither do I, and I look forward to more," he said as he stepped close beside her for a closer look at Junptra's beak that was turning berry red.

"Hey, you two," said Donika as she walked in.

Aria felt that her face turn as red as Junptra's beak.

"Hi, Mom."

"Wow, she is looking good, and already eating!"

"She was really lucky; she'll make a full recovery. I'll keep her overnight, and tomorrow she'll go to the Rescue Center. I'm worried about her chicks, though."

"They were fledging and looked healthy. I think the flock will help Juniper's mate take care of them."

"Junptra." Nikau and Aria corrected her at the same time.

Junptra gave a little squawk, with red juice dripping from her beak.

"Really, that's her kea name? Amazing how close that is to the name we gave her."

"Nikau said maybe they learned it from us when we named the chicks during the nesting study. Remember the mother kea perched nearby the whole time, like she was supervising?" said Aria.

"I wouldn't put it past them," said Donika.

Aria said, "I swear, they're getting smarter."

"They are," said Nikau.

They both looked at him. Aria said, "How do you know?"

"I reviewed the work of the directors before me. The scores of our annual intelligence tests on all rescued keas are higher every year. Other researchers are seeing the same thing, and we aren't sure what's happening or why. This weekend I'm presenting our results at a workshop at the Avian Intelligence Seminar at the Australian Ornithological Conference."

Aria said, "Hey, I'm going too. I'm meeting with veterinarians in conservation medicine and wildlife disease for a Wildlife Emerging Disease Forum. The biosecurity alerts have been low for a while, so I'm hopeful the conference will be in person."

They both looked at their phones and checked the pandemic app, MASCD. Nikau said, "Yep, the CDIT is still low between New Zealand and Australia and is forecast to stay that way through the next few weeks."

"You use MASCD, too," said Aria.

"Okay, translation here. What is MASCD and what is a CDIT?" asked Donika.

"Metrics, Alerts, Statistics, of Communicable Disease," is the latest Travel Communicable Disease Index app. It does a whole bunch of cool things, like, I can see the infectious disease markers for both countries are still in the green. Adelaide, here we come!"

"Well," said Donika, "I'll leave you to geek out on your phones. I've got a party to get ready for. See you both there. And, Junptra, I'll see you tomorrow at the Center. I'll get a small flight cage ready for you."

On her drive home, Donika dialed Isaac's room, and when he

didn't answer the room, the digital assistant picked up.

"I recognize your number as Donika Roberts. If this is correct, please say Isaac Roberts' birthdate for an update."

Donika said the date that was easy to remember—her spouse Kaleb's birthday also. The assistant said, "Patient is sleeping and stable. No surgery is planned. No internal bleeding or apparent concussion. Patient will stay overnight for monitoring and more tests."

"More tests for what?"

"Patient is scoring low on balance, unexplained by current blood-alcohol levels and accident trauma. Further tests are needed to assess his neurological state. Results will be available tomorrow. What else may I help you with?

"Please leave a message that Aria, Isaac's niece, will visit him tomorrow and to call if he needs anything."

"Accomplished. Goodbye."

At home Donika had thought she'd be tired, but tonight's kea gala was such a high point of the year that she felt like she was just gearing up for the day. She checked on Callum – only Aria called him by the endearment Kora. He was riding horses a year ago, and now couldn't get out of bed without assistance. They had run tests, but nothing definitive had been diagnosed other than atypical dementia. Some tests were still pending, but she didn't think much more could be known or done.

As she walked into Callum's room, where the home attendant, Joanie, was reading him a story, Callum looked up and rasped out, "Maggie – I – glad – home."

As she bent down to kiss him, she looked at Joanie who shrugged.

"It's Donika, Callum."

44

"But where Maggie?" He studied Joanie's face, looking for Maggie in her.

"Tell Maggie – talk more – about reseeding – upper pastures."

That had been a favorite project of his wife's, reverting the ranch back to native ecosystems after nearly two centuries of farming, which Donika had continued with resounding success. They helped sustain one of the largest kea flocks and the densest wildlife diversity on South Island. They kept sheep only for the educational experience for visitors, students, and interns.

"I'll go look for her. Joanie, why don't you come help me?"

"Tell Maggie I - miss - her."

In the hallway, Donika asked, "How is he today?"

"He was right in the middle of one of his hallucinations when you walked in. He was trying to get out of bed to get on his horse and was swearing at Maggie who laughed at him because his horse wouldn't stand still."

"That's exactly what Maggie would have done. I hope he finds solace in imagining she's still alive after all these years. But he got his hallucination right. He had a hard time mounting a horse right before we knew that something was seriously wrong."

"Any news on the additional tests?"

"Not yet. But they told us not to get our hopes up. In these kinds of cases it usually takes a biopsy to determine the exact cause of dementia."

"I better get back in case he tries to get out of bed to look for that ghost horse and ride off into the sunset. Uh, I mean..." she stammered, not meaning to allude to a terminal event.

"Don't worry about it. I know he's in rough shape. I'm so grateful for you. I haven't been here at all to help. Are you going to stay for the party, which – oh my gosh – starts in one hour?"

"I've seen the bustling volunteers all day. Everything should be set. I plan to come for a little while. A few volunteers offered to watch Callum. Let me run and check on him."

Indeed, the kitchen was a hive of activity and platters of food were filling up.

"*Kia ora*, everyone, and *tiki pali*," Donika greeted the mostly young volunteers, mixing three languages in one fell swoop, which she did when stressed.

"Kia ora," replied the chorus.

Closing the refrigerator door, Areta walked towards Donika. Areta was the oldest and longest serving volunteer, and in recent years had become paid staff of the KFC. She'd worked with Maggie and Donika and helped them raise Aria. Hugging each other, Areta looked closer at Donika. "I can see you've had one of those days. Let's go to the barn to make sure everything is set up. People will arrive soon. You can tell me all about it on the way."

Donika didn't get far in updating Areta when they stepped into the barn, long ago converted into a meeting hall they rented out for conferences, trainings, and even an occasional wedding.

Donika looked up at all the life-size, kea lights hanging from the ceiling. Turning in a circle, she saw potted native plants along the walls under Maori art. "*Dios mio*, you've done such a good job."

"It does look nice, doesn't it," said Michael adjusting a holographic projector system from a ladder. "The projectors and sound system are working. Which I guess means that they'll quit working during the evening." He hit play, and suddenly mountains surrounded them and flying keas filled the skies.

Michael, who volunteered as the current president of KFC, also owned Holistic Holograms.

"Wow," Donika said as other species of birds filled the sky. She smelled alpine meadow fragrances released from the projection system. "If we ever lose our birds, we could just use your system to keep the tourists happy."

Areta said, "Let's hope it doesn't ever come to that. We've been working too hard to save the kea and their ecosystem."

"Not hard enough," said Donika. "A kea was shot today close to Kowhai. Juniper. I mean Junptra."

"Oh no," gasped Areta. "I've known her since she was a chick. Did she survive?"

"She's with Aria recovering from surgery. Tomorrow she'll come for rehab. Could you prepare a small flight cage for her?"

"Let me go set that up now. And, Donika, you might want to fix up yourself as well."

"What? You don't think riding chaps and boots are gala attire?"

"They do fit our decoration motif. Wear whatever you think will appeal to our donors."

"I've got some sheep-dung-covered boots I can wear to match yours," said Michael.

"Okay," said Donika, "that's it. I'm going to change." She turned to leave, and the virtual keas swarmed to follow and swoop at her, as the sound system blared, "*Krrii-ah, krrii-ah!*"

LORAKIM JOYNER

Chapter 6
South Island New Zealand

Donika woke the next morning with a start, as she had been dreaming that the keas swirled above her. During the gala, guests had donated cash by holding up bills or checks that one of Michael's hologram keas dove to pick up. There were shrieks and laughter all around as a human volunteer instead pinched up the donations. The hanging kea lights flashed the amounts of texted donations. If ever there was a time for over-stimulation, it was during that part of the gala. It proved too much for Callum, who was wheeled in to accept for himself and on Maggie's behalf the life-time achievement award. He seemed to understand what was happening and enjoyed himself, until the keas started their fundraising dives. That had set him off, yelling and flailing in apparent horror. Those holo-keas of Michael's were too good for Callum. But they helped them meet their fundraising drive goals and then some.

Enjoying the comfort of her bed, Donika recalled other successes of the night. Aria and Nikau arrived late, but in time for both to give short presentations. Aria explained the latest results of her disease and health research with keas, and Nikau held the audience in thrall with his findings about kea intelligence and communication. Giggling now, but roaring with the others last night, she thought of Nikau describing how the research group lost one computer keyboard after another, researching what keas would do with a computer. The birds were more interested in tearing it apart than using it as a tool. So, instead, Nikau tried a holographic simplified key board that keas couldn't destroy, but could be manipulated with their dexterous feet and beaks. Some of the keas had learned to write sentences using images, and one typed English words. The result was a flock of kea couch-potatoes surfing the web and landing with high frequency on chef sites that featured 3D food preparation. Sometimes this species' behavior mirrored that of humans in startling detail.

Both Nikau and Aria had been a big hit at the party, and with each other, smiled Donika, recalling how much time they spent together. Now that she thought of it, they left together, too. If Aria could have even a little bit of what Donika had enjoyed with Kaleb, even for a short while, Donika could relax knowing that Aria would do more than work all hours of the day and night.

Thinking of hours in a day, Donika made her coffee the old-fashioned way without electronic sensors or timers. She peeked in and saw Callum sleeping, and then went to the Center's research room, nicknamed Kea Kontrol. She hit the switch to turn on a row of screens of live web cams at kea roosting, feeding, and nesting areas. The screen labeled number 14, the camera at Junptra's nest, was only a unified dark field. She thought the camera connection was bad, but a shimmer of light curled at the bottom of the screen. The camera was working, but not transmitting well. The screen for the meadow feeding area, number 5, was also dark, except for streaks of light.

She flipped on the master switch for all the screens. They

were all dark or mostly dark with moving white streaks. There was only one that showed a clear image, the one over the small flight training cage, just down the path from the house. Picking up her coffee, she knew it wasn't a glitch in the system, but something was definitely going on, and maybe had been for a while. Maybe something happened yesterday, while all the volunteers were busy preparing for the party. Everything was recorded and analyzed by the Kea Artificial Intelligence program (KAI). KAI processed thousands of hours of video every month, so Donika was certain that they'd figure out what happened. Live video had helped them understand kea behavior and communication, and raise funds and grow awareness. A couple of the cameras broadcast globally as Kea Kam.

She said, "KAI, play the last 24 hours of camera number 14 at twenty times normal speed and project onto the big screen."

"Good morning, Donika," replied KAI. "I understand."

On the big screen, there was Junptra and her mate, who they called Turtle. Donika could see he was the same large kea from the day before. He and Junptra had preened in the early morning sun before they flew off. A chick's head flashed on the screen, poking in and out of the nest entrance. Turtle landed alone near the entrance, where first one, then all three chicks joined him. When she lost sight of them, she said, "Switch to rear view camera 14." There, filling up the camera, was what looked like the entire flock. Then the image went dark.

"Computer, stop. Back up five minutes and play at normal speed."

She jumped at the sudden clamor of angry kea calls and voices. Turtle came into view, carrying her hat! He walked toward the camera with purpose in his eyes, lifted the hat, and then darkness again.

"Oh my god!" she heard a voice exclaim behind her. "Did that kea just purposely cover the camera with a hat?" said Christopher, a young, summer volunteer from the North Island. He looked like he could use a few more hours of sleep, but was excited. He said, "KAI, back up 30 seconds and freeze motion."

"Good morning, Christopher."

Leaning closer, he said, "Is that your hat? What's going on?"

"*Saber*! I have no idea. All the screens are out except for the one near our flight cage. I don't know how putting a hat on one camera makes them all quit working. Some light is getting through. KAI, go back twenty-four hours and play at twenty times speed video from camera number nine."

Materializing on the screen was the old kea's nest site. She wasn't out of her cavity yet. She couldn't roost like the others in trees. Instead, she slept in the old nest cavity where so many of her successful clutches had been documented. Keas were always visiting her, as was one now. They saw the visiting kea move toward the camera, and then it went dark.

"KAI, back up ten minutes of real time, and play at normal speed."

Both keas raised their wings and called *Krri-ah*. The visiting kea, who Donika now saw was Turtle, broke off a leafy branch. He carried it toward the camera, so all they could see was a sliver of the mountain slope through the leaves.

Christopher said, "He's blocking the camera, like in cam 14. I think it's Turtle. We haven't banded him yet."

"It is Turtle."

"Maybe he's found a new game?"

"Maybe," said Donika, but then she recalled the calculating

intent of the keas yesterday.

"Christopher, could you check all the cameras and see what happened? I need to check if the flight cage is ready for Junptra. Aria's bringing her up soon."

Donika walked out into the sun rising over the far peaks, which had much less snow than when she first arrived decades ago. Still, it was a beautiful sight that she never tired of. So entranced by the morning's light was she that she didn't notice the large kea perched in a tree over the flight cage. The tree's trunk blocked the camera's view of the kea. Walking up to the cage, she spilled her coffee with a sudden stop.

"Geez, Turtle, you about scared me to death. What are you doing here?"

"*Turagg, turagg,*" called the kea.

"Sorry, I can't pronounce your name, but I'll keep trying. Torgra. Truagara. Turtle. I guess you're stuck with it. So what are you up to? Keas rarely come down to the ranch. And what game are you playing with the cameras? It took us years to make them indestructible from your beaks, and you found another way to mess with us."

Turtle cocked his head left and right, concentrating on what Donika said. Donika had a sudden inspiration. "Did you sleep here last night waiting for Junptra to come back?"

Turtle made some chortling sounds, which were repeated from a distant tree.

"Oh, you brought your friends. Well, she'll be here in an hour."

Turtle called, "*Krrk, krrk,*" and he and a small flock flew toward the river.

"You have time for breakfast," she called after them. She

didn't know if the keas had a clear idea what she was saying, but they seemed to. She wanted others to see keas and all species as having inherent worth and dignity, so she always spoke to them with respect. They weren't objects; they were beings living in relationships.

She called Aria. "Can Nikau come with you? I've got something to show him that I need his input about."

"What's this about?"

"I'd rather show you both and get your impression without swaying you with my own impressions."

"I'll give him a call." She laughed that she couldn't lie. "Hell, mom, he's right here. Nikau, want to come to the ranch? Mom's being mysterious about something she needs your help with."

Donika heard garbled talking, then, "We'll be there soon. My assistant said Junptra had a good night and is ready to be moved. I hate letting her go so soon after surgery, but you'll take good care of her. And keas heal faster in their home territory."

"Just like people. Speaking of which, I need to take Callum for his daily ride around the house and garden. See you later."

An hour later, after walking with Callum, doing ranch chores, and topping off her coffee cup, she saw Aria's truck pull up. Aria got out with a small kennel holding Junptra, and Nikau carried a small bag of medications. They walked to the flight cage instead of stopping for coffee. Donika thought that Aria must have a busy day, packing for the conference and her flight tomorrow. New Zealand had been one of the country's most responsive to the climate emergency. Even though it was an island, Kiwis had drastically cut back on air travel. Now when people traveled off island, it was a big deal.

"*Morena*, Donika," said Nikau as he and Aria watched the

small flock of keas in the tree by the flight cage silently observing them, especially the kennel Aria carried. "Are those birds you've liberated from here?"

Donika said, "I recognize a few of them, but the others have never been here before."

"Do they often come here?"

"No, the flocks rarely come this low, not even in Maggie's time. That's part of what I want to ask you about. But let's get Junptra settled first."

Aria was already walking into the small flight cage that had double doors to keep keas from flying out when people entered. She walked through another door to a much smaller cage within the flight cage. She didn't want Junptra to stretch her healing flight muscles just yet. Junptra hopped out and called, "*Turagg, turagg!*" Turtle flew down to the cage. Through the cage wire, they clicked beaks, chortling. Then Turtle extended one leg through the wire cage wall, which Junptra grasped, and there they hung, united, as if one kea body with only cage wire separating them. Then the preening began, first their heads, and then Turtle, ever so carefully nuzzled around Junptra's bandaged chest. She responded, "Peep, peep."

Aria backed out of the cage to give them more privacy. Donika wiped a tear from her face, and Nikau filmed the birds

"This camera is still working, Nikau, so we can retrieve the footage."

"What do you mean 'still working'?" asked Aria as she clicked the cage's multiple combination locks and latches. They weren't worried about human theft, but they were about keas that studied humans and outsmarted them.

"Let me show you. And we'll give the keas some time alone."

Aria and Nikau brushed hands as they followed Donika into Kea Kontrol.

"*Morena*, Aria and Nikau. Donika, I was about to come get you," said Christopher, his face flushed. "You won't believe what I saw!"

Donika saw all the screens were frozen on an action, and each action was some version of the same thing, keas moving rocks, branches, leaves, and in one case a scrap of desiccated sheep skin, all placed over the field cameras.

Christopher said, "I asked KIA to go back twenty-four hours, starting with camera 14 at Junptra and Turtle's nest. After the keas covered up that camera, one-by-one all twenty-nine cameras were covered up. Some went dark at nearly the same time, so more than one flock was involved."

"Which means," said Nikau, "they taught others this behavior. They have stay focused on their task and ignored their daily regular behaviors. Donika, have you seen any other behavior pattern changes in the flock?"

Donika told them about Junptra's rescue by the flock and the subsequent kea-Isaac confrontation. She wasn't calling it an attack, to avoid projecting her own anger at Isaac on kea motivation. Maybe the keas' fight response was different from humans'. Or, she thought, at least different from her own attack inclinations.

Nikau said, "I want to study the recordings. Christopher, can you send me a link to the cloud recordings of the past twenty-four hours? I can review them along with KAI on our flight to Australia. Also, I can show them to some of my colleagues at the conference. It might be important to closely observe these flocks going forward."

Donika said, "We'll set up teams to clear the cameras and watch the screens live over the next few days," and looked to Christopher to confirm if this would work.

He said, "I think we can get enough volunteers, and you can fill in when needed," and looked at Donika who nodded.

"Speaking of the conference, I need to get a move on," said Aria. "Mom, here's Junptra's pain meds that you can titrate down if she seems comfortable, but keep her on antibiotics for a week. They're both extended release, so orally once a day. The meds are in a butter-flavored oil that she loves," she said as she pointed out fill-to-lines on each syringe. "Call me if she's not eating or moving much."

"Nikau, I'm going to say a quick goodbye to Kora," Aria said as Nikau was glued to the screens.

He studied the intense keas, their open beaks and erect head feathers, markers of intense and shared anger.

Chapter 7
South Island, New Zealand

Too excited and busy to sleep much, and with even less sleep the night of the kea party, Aria was on her third cup of coffee before it was light outside. She knew she wouldn't catch up on her sleep at the three-day conference, or want to. She'd have work to do and colleagues and friends to spend time with, and, she thought with a smile, Nikau to build a relationship with and all of Adelaide to discover. Plus, her good friend Jule might go.

For the fourth time, she checked MASCD, and still the TCDIT was green in both Australia and New Zealand. Large green bidirectional arrows between the countries gave her a warm feeling. Emerging diseases from wildlife was her area of interest, which is why she was distracted by what the rest of the map showed. As a girl she'd lost both her father and grandmother to the series of Covids, motivating her to earn a PhD in zoonotic diseases on top of her avian veterinary degree. She found every aspect of diseases fascinating.

The map flashed varying shades of yellow in the Northern Hemisphere and Central America for influenza season, and spots of orange for the eight-plus insect-transmitted diseases. The usual lockdowns for travel in multiple areas in Africa and Asia were in force, but thanks to increased surveillance and an international system of alerts and diagnostics, these threats were usually quickly resolved and travel was opened again. These interruptions were brief but frequent.

A clap of thunder overhead sparked her robo house assistant, Moana, to engage. "Good morning, Aria. There are approaching thunderstorms. Christchurch will experience flooding, especially along the Avon River. I see on your calendar that you are scheduled to drive to the Christchurch hospital this morning and then the airport. Do you want me to map out a route that bypasses the flooding?"

"That'd be great, Moana. I'll be ready in ten minutes."

"Would you like me to remind you what to pack?"

"Awesome idea again," she replied. "Watch me get the list 100 percent right."

"Toiletries – toothbrush, tooth paste, floss," Moana recited while Aria puttered in the kitchen.

"Technology – smart phone, smart watch, binoculars."

Aria's techno packing list was nearly as long as all her other items combined. It would have been longer but she'd upgraded to a smart holographic phone that projected a keyboard and worked off the cloud, so no more laptop.

"Clothes – two smart presentation shirts, smart swimsuit,'"

"Uh oh, one wrong." She'd forgotten her swimsuit. There usually wasn't time to visit local swim holes during conferences, but with Nikau along she'd make time for birdwatching and swimming, imagining a perfect day of Nikau, wild penguins, and parrots. And if Jule could fly in from Germany, her flex-ticket would allow her to stay a few more days to work and play with her.

Stepping out the door, she called, "Moana, place house on

extended away and start car." She saw on the car's internal halo screen Moana's route to the hospital, where she'd visit Isaac, was a squiggly mess of turns and backtracking. Every year, the flooding from climate change eroded the roads, although New Zealand had been on the forefront of high-level mitigation measures. She pressed the hospital icon on the screen and a bulletin flashed, "Risk of hospital visit today yellow, wear gloves and mask." She wondered what was going on, although having to glove and mask wasn't all that unusual. She guessed it was a patient with a respiratory virus that hadn't been typed yet. Her car was always stocked with gloves and masks for veterinary work and traveling. Her flight was still classified green, so she wouldn't have to wear personal protection equipment for the 4.5-hour flight.

Outside Isaac's room were staff and visitor gowns and masks, and the lights around the door flashed a mellow yellow. "*Morena*, Uncle Isaac. Hope I'm not too early," she said through a mask as she tied on a gown.

"Are you kidding? No hour is too early or late in a hospital. I must have been poked and prodded more than a flock of sheep during round up."

"What's up with the yellow alert? Have you been harassing the staff?"

"You know that's my specialty, but no, I've been a right good mate. Come give me a hug."

Aria looked over her shoulder for staff, she gave Isaac a quick but tender, crinkly sounding hug. Her mother wasn't on good terms with Isaac, but Aria loved him even though she didn't always understand him or approve of his actions.

"Mom told me the keas beat you up after you shot one. So

I'm pretty mad at you, too."

"I shot one? You know, I don't actually remember. There's a fuzzy memory of shooting my way out of what seemed like a three-ring circus of keas, but that had to be a dream."

"You don't remember? Wow, you must've knocked your head hard."

"That's what's strange. I didn't hit my head. That's why they're running all these tests. Something about neurological symptoms they can't explain from the accident, like ataxia and paresis.

Aria ran down her mental list of possible causes of lack of balance and weakness. She was suddenly riveted. She had to talk to the doctors.

"Isaac, can you appoint me to be your advocate so I can see what is going on?" she said as she stepped to the door.

"Already done. You're my advocate and have medical power of attorney. Can't think of a better caregiver than a bird doc! But don't go yet, I want to tell you something."

"Okay. Shoot."

"That's just it. I really don't believe I shot the kea. I quit doing that years ago. I know Donika doesn't believe me. Honestly though, I'm not sure what happened. I've been having such vivid daydreams that the doc called them hallucinations."

Alarms went off in her head. "That does it, Uncle Isaac. I am not going to the conference."

"Are you kidding? You could be just as good an advocate through your phone. I feel fine. Don't worry about me. Go. We'll keep in touch."

"Mom could check in on you," she said and then imagined her mother squinting at her.

"Not bloody likely."

"Why is it that you and mom don't get along?" she asked for the hundredth time in her life. "I know there were hard times when dad and grandma died, but you two always fought."

"I can't explain why I'm an asshole. Maybe I was jealous that Kaleb was so damn devoted to your mother. I loved him, too, you know. But in med school, we fought, and we were never the same after that."

"What did you fight about?"

"I can't even remember now, but I regret never talking about it with Kaleb or saying I was sorry. So I want to say to you I'm sorry I'm a piss-poor uncle. There might be something serious going on in my body, and I want you especially to know I love you. I care for you."

Now she was outright scared. Isaac was rarely serious, let alone transparently remorseful.

"Hell, you're great. And I love you, too."

But Isaac had dropped into an instant deep sleep, just like that. Lying flat and in a hospital gown, he looked so much like his father. Just like her Kora.

Aria rushed to the nurse's station, where there was only a Video Attendant. She spoke to the screen, "Review Isaac Roberts medical files."

"Look into the retinal scanner," droned the VA.

"Hello, Aria Roperta. Would you like to see the files now or do you want them sent to your smart device?"

"Please send them to my phone on file."

"Is there anything else I can help you with?"

The screen flashed options, and she clicked buttons to be updated on test results and patient's condition and to talk with the doctor today.

"Time?"

She raised her fingers to count the hours for travel and meetings. "This evening, after 6:00."

"The doctor has been informed. Sanitize your hands at the station near the exit."

On the way to the airport, Aria called Donika to update her on Isaac's condition. She didn't want to worry her, so she told herself not to say his symptoms were similar to Kora's. But her mother would probably guess that if she asked to see Kora's files. She asked anyway. "Mom, can you list me as advocate for Kora? I'd like to review his medical files and see if I can help."

Donika gave a too-quick, "Sure," which in turn made Aria leery. "Mom, are you okay? What's wrong? Is it Junptra? Kora?"

"Kora had another nightmare and woke up the house, and maybe the neighbors for miles. He's resting now. So is Junptra. Turtle and the flock spent the night near her, only leaving to feed at the river in the late afternoon. Turtle brought back berries and fed her through the cage. Watching them made me miss Papa."

Aria heard her mother's weariness, not just from lack of sleep but from so many years without her spouse, and all the other losses that had accumulated over a lifetime that spanned decades of unrelenting global crises. She had to stay focused for them both, as she had always done. "If Turtle's with Junptra, who's taking care of their chicks?"

"Yesterday theirs was the first camera we uncovered. We briefly saw other keas feeding the chicks."

"Briefly?"

"The keas covered each camera again after we left. They're all dark this morning."

"What are they up to? Seems like they don't want us watching them."

"We'll have to go back to observing them the old-fashioned way, in person. We're sending some people up today to check on the last nests to fledge chicks. From what little we could observe, the flock is preparing to fly to their summer grounds. Maybe by next nesting season, they'll be tired of playing games with the cameras."

"Hey, Mom, I'm at the airport. Gotta go."

"Have a good and safe time. See you next weekend."

Aria breezed through security, her smart watch relaying her various physiological parameters automatically. The line was longer for those who didn't have the technology and had to be scanned. It was a minor inconvenience compared to having the entire world shut down.

Approaching the gate, she saw Nikau at the window, looking like he was signing messages to the black-headed and black-billed gulls flying past. As she got closer, she saw that he was typing on his holo keyboard. Perhaps he was doing both, his split attention to both work and the gulls a form of saying, "I love you." At least that's what every hour of her own life said to birds and wildlife.

"Kia ora, Nikau," Aria greeted Nikau with a peck on the check, unsure how he handled public affection. He embraced and twirled her as if they'd been apart for months and together for years, instead of only days on both accounts.

"Kia ora to you. How is your family?"

"Junptra is fine, but I'm worried about Isaac. He's on yellow alert at the hospital for undiagnosed neurological symptoms."

"I'm surprised they let you travel, as strict as the

government's been lately."

"Well, it's only a yellow alert, and pale-yellow at that. I had my smart phone and watch with me, so MASCD knew I visited the hospital and determined I was okay. Find anything interesting on the kea recordings?"

"KIA is still running the programs. As fast as our computer system is, it still takes hours to go through all the cameras, searching for words and word phrases. It should have finished by now, but KIA picked up some new word combinations I haven't heard before either." He pointed to some sonograms displayed in a smaller window and handed her his ear plugs. She smiled at hearing kea calls and at Nikau's intimate gesture of sharing.

"I mean, we knew that keas and other parrots make up new phrases that have meaning to them, but this is the first time we've seen such a rapid increase of novel phrases in a wild flock." He pointed to a graph. "See how the novel phrases in English plotted for our captive keas have slowly increased over the decades? And here's the graph for the wild keas using their natural vocalizations. It's almost a level line until the last several years. Both the wild and captive flocks are using verbal language more. What's interesting is that the increasing curves are matching the rise in intelligence performance results. That's what I think anyhow. With using various methodologies and researchers over the years, it's hard to determine the consistency of the data as some seems a bit squishy..." he trailed off. "Speaking of squishy," he said as he squeezed her hand, "I'm sorry I'm droning on. Tell me what's going on with Isaac."

"I don't know. I'm going to review his medical records on the plane," she said, holding up her phone, "and see if anything jumps out at me, or at least be prepared to help him make decisions. And just so you know, I can't think of a better way to be greeted than to be hugged, twirled, and courted with kea calls and research."

Nikau smiled and Aria smiled even bigger. They lapsed into a comfortable silence that continued through the boarding process and early part of the flight. They concentrated on their work until snacks were served.

Nikau asked, "How's your presentation coming? Tell me your topic again."

"I'm part of a panel that's reviewing infectious and zoonotic diseases in birds. A tremendous amount of avian research, and in all wildlife, is monitoring possible emerging zoonotic diseases. We reviewed recent and early research to see where we should direct future studies. I'm in charge of the 'P' diseases."

"'P' diseases?"

"So many infectious agents have 'P' names in parrots: Psittacosis is the best known, but also Polyoma, Pacheco's like Herpes viruses, Parvoviruses, Poliovirus, Parainfluenza, and Prions."

"I thought birds didn't get prion disease."

"Right, they don't get the disease, but they have prion proteins they can mechanically transmit and infect other animals, such as crows that feed on infected carrion and then transport it to another area."

"That's scary!"

"Not so much. Though it's been documented that crows who scavenge carcasses can carry the prions from one area to another, there's never been direct transmission from birds to humans. And in New Zealand, we don't have any current cases of transmissible prion disease in humans or any other species."

"Then why study it?"

"Because every few years we discover a new prion disease in wildlife. It's only a matter of time before one becomes infectious to people, like BSE."

"BSE?"

"Bovine spongiform encephalopathy. Mad Cow Disease."

"Oh yeah. The zombie disease that comes from eating cow brains which makes you walk and talk funny and be crazy," said Nikau.

"Wait, do you watch zombie movies?"

Nikau experienced this as a test. If he said no and she did like them, then she'd be disappointed. And if he said yes and she didn't, she might think less of his intellectual prowess. His face relaxed in accepting that their relationship, if theirs was heading anywhere and he hoped it was, could not be based on a lie. "Yes."

"I see. And what is your favorite one?" she said, slightly frowning.

He had no clue where this was going. "There's so many sub-genres to choose from."

"So, you are a zombie geek then?" When Nikau stayed silent, she said, "I usually prefer the alien dystopic zombie genre, but any zombie film will do in a pinch."

"You've got to be kidding me!"

"No, siree. In fact, I have over 100 stored in the cloud. We could watch one right now. Shall we?"

"How about Warm Bodies?"

"Okay, a Rom-Zom-Com. Cuing it up," she said

Aria handed him one of her ear plugs, returning Nikau's earlier gesture. They smiled that this was a better trip than they imagined, like a romance travel flick, or one that started like a romance with vague zombie undertones, then exploding into a full-on zombie apocalypse.

LORAKIM JOYNER

Chapter 8
South Australia

By the time the plane swung over St. Vincent Gulf to land at Adelaide, they'd finished the film, while intermittently responding to their Cloud Correspondence.

"That was a lot of CCs. My head was in the clouds more than in the plane," said Nikau, flirting before he noticed that Aira still had her ear plugs in.

Walking from the airport to the Metro stop, they were hit with a wave of heat, which they didn't notice because a flock of sulfur-crested cockatoos landed in a tree in the median. Nikau fell back into his scientist observer mode, noting the position of their crests and other feather facial features.

"Boy, they sure are relaxed birds in this relatively human-dense environment," he said, craning his head backwards to keep them in view as the bus pulled out.

Aria pointed forward. "Look!" They saw white wisps and large white clouds everywhere.

"Are those all cockatoos? I knew the populations of parrots were increasing here, but I had no idea they were so dense in urban areas."

Aria said, "Where my mother's from, it's often the urban

areas that are the last refuge for endangered parrots because cities have less hunting and trapping, and, ironically, more food. But I think more is going on than that."

"Those aren't just sulfur-crested cockatoos, but also corellas and galahs!"

"This is like nature's Disneyland, made possible by the passing of the Fly Free laws five years ago."

He said, "That's when I was buried in my PhD dissertation and rarely saw our own New Zealand parrots."

"The Fly Free laws came out of the Unconditional Solidarity Movement that's strong in Southern Australia. Before the laws, you could keep some Australian birds for pets, now you can't. But it's hard to believe that in just a decade so many birds could propagate. Some people who had birds in the home let them go to see them fly free. And maybe it was fallout from the Corona Years. People realized the wildlife trade could be a health threat."

Nikau said, "Are you going to the US reception tonight?"

"I might be late, because our Emerging Disease group meets for roundtables, and I have an appointment to talk to Isaac's doctor. But I should be there by the time they break into the various country and regional subgroups."

They arrived at the hotel, one of the new, green, outbreak-resistant, dormitory-style conference centers. It had small individual rooms that allowed for social distancing and multiple larger rooms for gatherings, or to take part via holographic presentations.

"Okay, I'll see you tonight. The Avian Intelligence group roundtables start in an hour."

In her room, Aria reviewed Isaac's and Kora's medical files. Both showed neurological abnormalities, including loss of balance and cognitive deficiencies. The brain MRIs showed significant deterioration in Kora and less so in Isaac. The list of possible diseases that could cause this was long, and what was causing Isaac's symptoms could be completely different from Kora's, especially given the age difference. Both could also have atypical dementias caused by different etiological agents. She noticed that both had had spinal taps and that the results were pending for Isaac and were negative for Kora. Not much to go on, though she thought of more tests for Kora. "Moana, remind me to ask Isaac's doctor when he calls about running further tests."

"I will, and welcome to Australia!"

Kiia-ah rang her phone loudly as it automatically connected to the room's interactive systems. She cut her already short shower by five seconds. Much of Australia was undergoing a decade's long draught, and water was regulated tightly. The message flashed on the all-purpose wall screen: *Just arrived. Meet me in the bar before the meeting starts? Jule.* Aria hurried to dry off and pull on clothes. Theirs was mostly a holo friendship, ignited several years ago when Jule was doing a survey of the pathology of infectious diseases of wild parrots in Australia, which complemented Aria's survey of disease in the parrots of New Zealand.

Screeching like teenagers, their hug was almost as long as Aria's shower. A few heads turned in their direction, probably at least one of the staring strangers thinking what beautiful babies those two could have. Aria was naturally a dark bronze from her indigenous lineage on both sides of her family, Maori and Miskitu, with dark hair that flowed like curving rivulets down her shoulders, even more so when damp from the shower. Her blue eyes, from her Western European ancestors, matched Jule's, whose tanned skin complimented her Scandinavian golden-blond hair. One short, one tall, both outdoorsy and athletic, and both shining with curiosity and intelligence.

"How long has it been?" asked Jule, her German-Aussie accent endearing to Aria's ears.

"What? Is that the first thing we talk about? Next we'll start sharing all our ailments and how bad our memories are."

"I thought we could try to be normal people before talking nonstop for three days about the latest PCR tests and population counts of parrots."

"We're going to talk about penguins too, right? And see them?"

"Yes! I finagled permits to collect samples for a picornavirus survey after the conference."

"I can't wait because penguins have almost as many 'P' diseases as parrots do. There's the picornos, paramyxos, and the pingus."

"We are the 'PP' sisters for sure!"

Speaking of 'PP,' I'm going to take a bathroom break."

"So soon?"

"Maybe I've got a touch of a bladder infection."

Jule said, "I see. You'll have to tell me all about your new romance when you get back."

"Oh please," said Aria. Jule could always read her so well.

After finishing their beers, they went to the roundtable discussion on emerging diseases. They were amazed at the number of people. Sure, 75% of them were holoed in, but the technology was such that the room seemed filled, and provided simultaneous translation at the same time. Jule and Aria spent a rousing hour moving between the tables discussing diseases and greeting colleagues who represented every continent on Earth and over 100 countries. They met at the exit on their way to the Unconditional Solidarity meeting. Just inside the US reception room, Aria saw Nikau talking with colleagues. Jule and Aria joined the circle, and the conversation lagged.

"Oh, sorry, we didn't mean to interrupt," said Aria.

"No, please join us," said Nikau.

Introductions were quickly made before the room's engagement system boomed and sent all the phones a rhythmic vibrating cadence to the theme song of US, "US with the Earth," a takeoff on the old song, "We are the World."

A voice at the front of the room said, "Welcome, everyone. By being here, you make US stronger. Please join in welcoming each other by singing along to the video. We welcome each other so that we can be welcoming to every individual on Earth! Take the song of liberation into your heart, and as the video plays, see who is no longer on the planet because we didn't welcome them as US."

Every wall and even the ceiling filled with images of species that had gone extinct, and indigenous peoples whose cultures and homes had been destroyed. Aria recognized the Moa and the Kakas of New Zealand, and she and Jule reached for each other's hand when the orange-bellied parakeet flashed by. They had worked to save that species but had been unsuccessful. The images flashed faster and faster because extinction was accelerating.

The key of the song changed as the images of extinction shifted to images of people helping other people and animals. Aria thrilled to see a photo of her grandmother in the collage. By the end of the video, there were wet eyes and cheers as the last words repeated, "US with Earth!"

"So now we know who is not in the room with us, but forever with us in our hearts. Take a moment to look around the room to see who is in the room. US. We are the ones who vow to be in Unconditional Solidarity with all of life on Earth, and with all individuals. Each of us lives this vow in our own ways, but all go in the same direction. It's not an easy path, and we need company to help us hold the beauty and tragedy on the journey. We have tables set up around the room, and you can key in a holo to shine above that calls people to your region or your particular passion. Witness to each other, and, if so called, refine your vow now to specific actions. There are no rules, just compassion and commitment. Have faith in yourselves. Ready? Go!"

The room erupted in chaos as people rushed to tables to key in images, bumping into each other as they craned their heads upwards to find familiar geographic regions or species. At one table, a flock of parrots swirled overhead. Aria got so excited she tripped and fell. Jule and Nikau helped her up and followed her as she rushed to the parrot table. Jule stopped at the table where penguins were surfing in the ocean, and Nikau couldn't resist the ravens croaking at a corner table. Aria looked around at all the images, deciding where to go next. Her hand covered her heart when the Apu Mountains of La Moskitia rose out of the lowland mist. This was her mother's land, where Aria spent a year with her cousin Kendi, volunteering to help with the now-famous parrot conservation project, Apu Pauni. She claimed La Moskitia as her land, as the people and parrots there had claimed her.

Music slowly rose above the conversations of various species in various languages, and the images faded and the gathered hushed. A voice said, "You have heard each other's calling to serve life, and the many species and peoples calling out to you. This reception has now ended, but your service to life has just begun, and begins again and again with every breath. Now be faithful. Go!"

Aria looked for Jule and Nikau for a group hug that attracted more and more people, until it was a room hug, along with holos, bringing the numbers to thousands holding each other to their hearts and vows. The long moment shifted. Arms dropped, and hands reached for buzzing phones. Aria expected a copy of the regional and species vows that had been recorded with links so they could find each other during the conference and beyond, but it was MASCD buzzing an alert. New Zealand was now a pulsing orange circle. She zoomed in and saw the alert centered on Christchurch Hospital, where Isaac was. She flipped through the app but found no explanation for it. She saw a message from Isaac's doctor with a callback number.

"I gotta go, guys. It's Isaac's doctor. I'll find you later." She walked away saying, "Moana, call the last number," as she walked outside.

"Calling now and remember to ask the doctor about additional tests."

"Hello, Dr. Jennings here."

"Kia ora. Dr. Ropata calling. Isaac's niece and advocate."

"Are you a human doctor?"

"Veterinarian. What's going on? MASCD is centered over your hospital. Is it Isaac?"

"I'm afraid so. The spinal tap revealed the presence of an unknown brain-derived protein. Do you know what that means?"

"I know what it suggests in nonhuman species, including the

presence of prions. But what does it mean for Isaac?" Aria knew the answer but tested the doctor.

"I can't say for sure with his symptoms, but I've scheduled a battery of further tests."

"Including PMCAs," she said, hard and clinical.

"Yes, those specifically."

"That's why the lockdown then. You don't know what kind of prion it is, if it's one at all."

"Yes, it's a precaution. There could be a genetic cause, or it could be idiopathic. And we can't rule out a prion origin from another species."

"How's Isaac doing?"

"He's stable. The results just came in. He's sleeping, so I haven't told him. But we'll wake him to move him to the isolation ward. You can call him in an hour, after we get him settled."

"I will. And please message me as soon as you get the results."

"You and everyone else in New Zealand. People really don't want a repeat of what happened in the UK last century with BSE, and in Colorado a decade ago with the spongiform encephalopathy in deer and elk."

Aria's exhalation betrayed her.

He said, "I don't mean to frighten you with what might not happen."

"It's okay. I know about those outbreaks. My PhD was on zoonotic diseases, with an emphasis on emerging wildlife diseases. I've studied prions for years."

"Great. I look forward to you helping us think this through and taking care of Isaac. Goodbye, Dr. Ropata."

"Bye." She didn't suggest that he call her Aria. She wanted

him to be his best and hear what she had to offer. Too often, human doctors, at least those mired in the past, didn't think veterinarians knew their stuff. She didn't want to risk Isaac's health with a stranger's bias.

"Over here, Aria," Nikau called as Aria returned inside.

Jule asked, "Aria, what is it? Is Isaac okay?" "They think he has a prion disease."

They all hugged in silence. They knew too well that prion diseases were universally fatal. No cure.

LORAKIM JOYNER

Chapter 9
South Australia

"Whoop, whoop," sang out Aria's phone too early. She'd reset it to the call of the fairy penguin, thinking when in Australia she'd do as the Australians do. But now she thought it was too early to hear it or for a phone call, though it was three hours later in New Zealand.

"Hi, Mom. What's up?"

"Quite a bit I'd say. I got your message last night about Isaac having some test results."

"They're running a battery of PMCAs, and we should get the results today."

"Aria, in English or Spanish, please?"

"They're Protein Misfolding Cyclic Amplification tests that look for prions."

"Oh, right, your PhD topic. But what's that got to do with Isaac?"

"He might have a prion disease, Mom."

"I thought you said animals have prions all the time."

"They do, but some are particularly harmful for certain species. For instance, sheep get scrapie and humans get vCJD, Variant Creutzfeldt-Jakob disease, which is also known as Mad

Cow Disease."

"But we don't have either of those diseases here."

"There are other prion diseases, and the tests could be wrong. It takes more than just a spinal tap showing abnormal proteins and symptoms to diagnose a disease. All we can do is wait and see what happens. Do you want me to come home?"

"Come home? Why would you do that? Isaac is stable, isn't he?"

Aria said, "Yes, but I don't want to get stuck in Australia," but guiltily thought if she had to, how better to spend it than with Jule and Nikau.

"Why would you get stuck there? What's going on?"

"Mom, you really do need to update the apps on your phone and get MASCD for notices. Christchurch is on orange alert because Isaac might have a disease that could be communicable. Prion diseases are communicable, but usually only through ingestion or exposure to infected tissue."

"I was out all day yesterday. I didn't get any news. That's what I wanted to talk to you about."

"What, Kora?"

"No, Junptra. She's gone."

"She died?"

"No. I got up this morning and the cage doors were open, with no Junptra. The flock that had been roosting here was also gone. I checked the camera recordings to see who was responsible, but the feed cut out late last night. I checked the outdoor camera and the cables had been chewed through, like kea-chewed, not cut."

"How could they chew or out think us through all the fail safes for the cage? It was kea-proof."

82

"Well, apparently not. They were attentive to our comings and goings with Junptra. I thought it was because they cared for her. But looks like they were learning how to get in the cage."

"They're smart. But memorizing two combination locks?"

"I guess it could have been a person stealing Junptra, but the locks weren't damaged, just open. Perhaps an inside job? My instinct says Junptra wanted to go and the flock wanted her out of there."

"I hope she was ready for movement with her injury."

"She was doing well, but I was worried, so I sent out the drones yesterday to the usual feeding areas and nest sites. I never saw any keas, and one of the drones crashed near a nesting area. I rode out on Aras and found the drone. It was chewed up, but no keas. They're just gone. Like the ones in Christchurch."

"What?"

"When I filed a missing kea report at the police department, the detective said they were swamped with reports of kea thefts. Someone broke into KFC and either stole or released all the keas. Some zoos and collections reported missing keas yesterday and last night."

"Do you think that a smuggling ring is rounding up keas for illegal trade?"

"It's hard to imagine that thieves are that organized, though they have sophisticated methods, especially when it comes to the illegal wildlife trade. But the alternative is a deep kea plot."

Aria smiled at that.

Her mother said, "Stay where you are and check in throughout the day. How's the conference going?"

"It's so great. Jule is here, and the US gathering last night was inspirational. If I wasn't so worried about Isaac, Kora, and the missing keas, I'd be having a wonderful time. Speaking of, I need to get moving to make the morning sessions."

"Okay. *Te amo!*"

"*Aroha*, Mom!"

Aria met Jule and Nikau for breakfast at the hotel café, each slapping one another with the US handshake, and then doing a three-way. Heads turned, some in solidarity, some irritated because they thought the US movement extreme, and more than one thinking that those three could make beautiful babies together. Nikau's feature and form seemed to highlight the DNA of several continents: Africa, Europe, Asia, and Maori and other Pacific Islanders, complementing the other two. But it was perhaps their focused presence with one another that drew the most notice.

"Nikau," said Aria before they sat, "the keas are gone!" She could have texted him the news earlier, but as part of the conference guidelines, they were committed to using their technology as little as possible in deference to in-person interactions.

At the same time, Nikau said over Aria, "You won't believe what our group came up with last night."

"What?" all three said.

"You first, Aria. What about the keas?"

"Junptra got out, probably liberated by the kea flock, and there's been a rash of kea disappearances all over New Zealand. There's no proof yet if keas were responsible."

"Well, I might have some," said Nikau.

"What?" they said.

"After the US meeting last night, our working group met, and every single participant reported an increased complexity in kea communication, as well as higher performance in problem solving and intellectual tasks. The keas are approaching an Intellectual Index of 5."

The Index, or II, used a complicated algorithm to adjust for species' specific expressions of intelligence and communication, as well as neural-tissue type and processing, neural-tissue weight/body weight ratios, and the results of standardized tests. It was an attempt to move away from human intelligence as the gold standard. Instead, intelligence was mostly rated in comparison to conspecifics or other closely related species.

"So, are you saying that maybe they are coordinating and hiding their movements, so they can release caged keas?" asked Jule.

"Applying Occam's razor of parsimony, what is the simplest explanation? Coordinated keas or coordinated kea thieves?" posed Aria.

They were silent, reading each other's eyes. Nikau said, "Yup, we don't have enough information yet. I'll share this with my group today. It's a great foundation for discussing our recent work. And I've got an uncle in the police who can get us more information, too."

Aria said, "Okay. We gotta run. Our session is starting."

"Good luck with your 'PP' presentation!"

Jule and Aria walked into the room just as the morning facilitator stood up. They found seats not occupied by holo attendees.

"Good morning, everyone," began the morning facilitator.

Aria and Jule recognized her as Dr. Helga Constantin, an avian veterinarian who had been practicing avian conservation medicine for over 40 years, on projects both successful and non.

85

Jule knew her from the last days of trying to save the orange-bellied parakeet in Australia, and Aria from working with her on the Kakapo, a New Zealand endangered parrot whose numbers never rose over 300 after getting hit with one disease after another. Dr. Constantin had raised funds to train field biologists and veterinarians all over the world and had provided both pathology and other diagnostics services to far-flung places on Earth.

"We begin this morning with a review of avian disease, with an emphasis on zoonotic diseases. In the afternoon we will consider any emerging trends, and this evening we'll break into roundtables to discuss directions our research should go. I want to give a special shout out to our guests from the Zoonotic Global Surveillance Consortium and the International Emerging Zoonotic Disease Working Group, and – oh heck, why don't you each just write what group you are from and place it in the chat? I don't want to leave anyone out. The list of attendees is impressive. The best minds and most recognized working groups in the world are here."

Realizing this awed Aria as she settled in for Dr. Constantin's first presentation, "Pathogen Strains in Strained People, Wildlife, and Ecosystems."

"There is no one here who doesn't know the crisis Earth has experienced for decades. We are well into the sixth extinction, our ecosystems are debilitated, the climate shifts are an emergency, and the lowering biodiversity, except in some remaining isolated pockets, has led to the unprecedented emergence of wildlife suffering, diseases, and zoonotic threats for the human global community. More than 60% of human disease can be spread from other animals, and more than 75% of new emerging human diseases have their origins in other animals. Millions of people have died in the last two decades, though with our global surveillance system we have improved outcomes for many of the outbreaks. Most of the more serious emergent diseases come from other mammals, so why the emphasis on birds? It's because we care about ourselves and want to be prepared, and especially because we care about birds. We don't want more birds to go extinct because of infectious disease. Those of you from North America know about the Carolina Parakeet, and that the work with the de-extinction process resulted in strong evidence that a paramyxovirus struck down the remaining Carolinas. Fragmented and stressed populations are prone to disease, and that unfortunately describes many of today's wild animals. The orange-bellied parakeet was lost to circovirus, as was the cape parrot and echo parakeet. And we have several other endangered parrot populations with high mortality rates because of this virus and others. With our knowledge of transmissible diseases, we have been careful to translocate and reintroduce parrots from one region to another, and if we do, we do as extensive a screening as possible. We also rely on community conservation, attempting to conserve the species through local efforts without having to undertake the risky and expensive release of parrots that might have been exposed to a known contagion, or for that matter, to a disease agent we are not aware of. A prime success story is that of the sun parakeet in Guyana and Brazil. Indigenous villages, where the last birds were found, committed to the conservation of this species. Through monitoring and protection, the parakeets rebounded from a couple of hundred to over 20,000, all without having to bring in a single parakeet from another region or implement a captive breeding program. Unfortunately, such successes are rare. We now exist in fragmented and stressed populations, and we don't want to lose one more species, for their sake and for ours. Parrots as seed dispersers are the farmers of the forest. If we lose them, we lose the health of the forest, and we all lose."

Aria, though moved by the sentiment, had heard this presentation a couple of times and so, not meaning to, tuned out with the distraction of Isaac's condition, and dozed. Moana vibrated in her pocket and woke her. She saw two incoming alerts, one from Dr. Jennings and one from MASCD. Jule raised an eyebrow as Aria scooted by her and out the door, unable to keep from stepping on some holo toes, though no one seemed to mind.

"Hello, Dr. Jennings? That was quick turnaround on the PMCAs. It usually takes a lot longer to get results from our parrot samples."

"Yes, I read up on your work and am quite impressed, Dr. Ropata. You've done a lot of research on interspecies prions. I put a rush on it because I'm not sure Isaac's case is an isolated one."

"What do you mean? What did the tests show?"

"He's definitely got a variant prion in his neurological system, but we don't know what kind yet or the origin. I've seen similar cases recently in New Zealand, where there hasn't been a clear previous diagnosis. We'll have to do contact tracing, beginning with you, and anyone else in your family. We also need to do genetic testing. I've already asked your mother. Excuse the question, but do we need to do genetic testing with you, Dr. Ropata? Your last name is different, so I wasn't sure if you were biologically related."

"We are. My parents named me the Maori equivalent of Roberts."

"Oh, I see. So, do I have your permission to take a look at some of your banked genetic material at the South Island Genetic Bank?"

"Yes, of course. You are looking for CJD?"

"Yes, we need to check for genetic causes, both inherited and acquired, though it doesn't present much like that."

"Would you please run the PMCAs on my grandfather, Callum Roberts? He's had a sudden onset of neurological signs and his spinal tap was negative, but perhaps they missed something. And they didn't run PMCAs."

"That's a smart idea, Dr. Ropata."

"Thanks. And you can call me Aria."

"And I'm Luther. "

Before going back into the room, Aria filled out her contact tracing survey, and sent off quick messages to her mother and Isaac. She wasn't too concerned because prions transmission from human-to-human had never been documented. Even if lockdown was necessary, it would probably be for only a short time.

As Aria walked back into the room, Helga was finishing her presentation. Jule showed her phone to Aria, where MASCD had sent her a contact tracing survey to fill out, and gestured for Aria to look at the room as she sat down. Many heads bowed and fingers subtly punched holo keyboards. Helga noticed.

"Excuse me, what's happening?"

Aria stood to explain when Helga reached into her pocket to pull out her vibrating phone.

"Oh, I see. It looks like the conference is on lockdown due to some possible wildlife transmitted disease in New Zealand. And I see Dr. Ropata from New Zealand is looking, excuse me, a little sheepish. Care to explain?"

"Yes, my uncle has the presence of some kind of prion in his system and is suffering neurological effects. I visited him before coming to the conference. As it's of prion origins, I imagine this is just a temporary precaution. Sorry, everyone."

"Well, we won't let this set us back. This building is set up to continue to hold the conference in holo mode. Why don't we take an extra-long coffee break so everyone can finish the survey and get situated in your rooms. Our next talk will be from Dr. Ropata at 10 a.m. I see hotel management in the back of the room, if you have any questions for them. Yes, Dr. Mbungo?" Helga addressed him formally, although they worked together for many years in his home region, now called the United Kongo Republics.

"I know this was organized as an experiential conference, so let me just ask, are we being setup to work with emerging diseases by pretending that there is an outbreak?"

"No, this is not a drill. But I wish I'd thought of that. I'll see you in 30 minutes."

Jule caught Aria's arm and pulled her from the crowd. "Listen, I hardly ever get to see you in person, and maybe this is going to go on for a while. Want me to ask the hotel if we can get an isolation suite instead of individual rooms?"

"Ah, Jule, I don't want to give you anything, though prions, if that what it is, aren't transmissible except usually by ingesting body parts."

"Come on, it will be like a slumber party."

"Can I join?" Nikau asked, walking up.

Aria said, "That'd be great. Jule?"

Jule said, "In for a penny in for a pound, I always say."

"As long as we're going with the P alliterations, we'll be the 'PP' Suite," said Aria.

Nikau, tilting his head, said, "Hmm?"

"Pajama party!"

LORAKIM JOYNER

Chapter 10
La Moskitia, Honduras

Almost half a world away, Aria's cousin Kendi was also thinking of parties, but of the political variety. Distracted, she hadn't noticed the large parrots gathering silently above her in the forest patch. If she had seen them, she would have been startled. Usually the scarlet macaws near the villages were quite vocal, especially the juvenile flocks that seemed hell-bent on making trouble. The only other liberated animals that were worse were the monkeys and the yellow-naped amazons. The village had long ago lost confidence that they would ever eat another coconut or orange grown from their trees, and mangos that once dropped like rain from the sky were now only for the ingenious foragers who could find them, where the wild animals had not. The villagers didn't seem to really mind, gladly trading the fruit for the returning abundance of parrots that the elder among them had seen only as very small children. The ancient ones told of their grandparents who had seen even greater concentrations of all manner of species in this land of savanna and broadleaf forest.

Kendi ducked when wings of bright red blocked her view as dozens of scarlet macaws swooped down at her. At the last minute, they veered away, though some wing tips and toes mussed her hair. The air cracked with the beat of wings, as well as the ear-piercing calls that evolved to carry through thick forest and over long distances.

"*Pana nani*! What are you doing sneaking up on me like that?" she called after them as she swept the strands of her hair from her face and shielded her eyes from the sun to see them. Though she'd grown up in a village with more parrots than people, she never tired of their glossy red and yellow wings in the evening light. Their nearly nonstop mischievous and raucous bickering, however, was sometimes enough to make her want to join her aunt in New Zealand. But from what her cousin Aria had said, the keas were even worse, not as loud but more destructive.

"Grraureck," the scarlets screamed nonstop as they looped above her into the village.

"I wish my people would be as happy to see me," she said and returned to her reflections on the federation meeting she'd attended in Kirtira, a larger village upriver. The topic before them was whether to officially become part of the Communitarian Nations of Miskitu, comprised mostly of their neighboring Nicaraguan villages. Others, perhaps the more Western leaning residents, wanted to merge with the Renewed Republic of Central America, the first union having disbanded in 1841. Still others whispered of a Miskitu Kingdom, beholden to no one. Kendi imagined such a scenario as she counted her bloodline back to Miskitu kings through her maternal line. Another meeting would be necessary to make a decision.

"Mama!" cried teenage Lapta. Her oldest ran to wrap her arms around her. "I'm glad you're home!"

"Me, too."

Besides her daughter, the guaras, or scarlet macaws, squawked welcome like they were family. In a photo of Kendi as a baby, she shared a hammock with a rescued guara chick. Now she smiled at several perched above her, including her old friend Rak, who was her age. She gestured a flying motion, and Rak swooped down to Kendi's outstretched arms. With a chortling guara on one arm and a chattering teen on the other, the multispecies family approached the biggest stilted home in Kaskatara, inherited from her mother, along with the farm lands along the Wastu River. When she was a child, her house had been a refuge for countless siblings, cousins, and extended family from Nicaragua, and parrots that were cared for by her mother until they could fly free. She felt the stab of missing her mother, and also her papa and Orlin. "Are you okay, Mama?"

"Pain, pain. I was thinking of how much I missed your *dama* and *kuka*."

"Me, too, Mama. When's Papa coming home?"

Before she could answer, her son Keruto shouted from the top of the stairs, "Mama! See what I've been coloring!" The five-year-old held up a colorful drawing of two macaws, one red and one green, the great green macaws now extinct in Honduras.

"They are so beautiful!" she said, smiling for him, while mourning the great greens. The green macaws were already scarce when she was a child, but relentless poaching for the prized birds and the destruction of the forest where the great greens nested had sealed their fate. Kendi kicked off her shoes and scaled the steps into her home, as her sister-in-law Yessenia greeted her at the top. Rak flew toward the tall pines north of the village. "Grraurek, grraurek," called the macaws in the trees. One followed Rak and offered a few calls before silently flying with her, wing tip to wing tip.

"How was the meeting?" asked Yessenia, wiping her hands on the towel over her shoulder.

"Well, no one got killed. So that's something. It was tense. They postponed any decisions to let tempers cool, but we can't wait much longer. They want us back next week. I hate to have to ask you to look after the kids again."

Her sister-in-law glanced knowingly at her before saying, "You don't want to leave too soon," with a smile she couldn't hide. She pulled Kendi away from the children and into the kitchen that was hot from stoked embers. Yessenia whispered, "I got a message from Jaora's wife. They're thinking of coming home."

Kendi couldn't help gasping from fear, mixed with joy. She called to the children, "Keruto, Lapta, fill up the water jugs at the creek for dinner."

"What are you making? And what's in your bag? It looks big," Keruto asked, glancing up from coloring

"It's a surprise. I did a little bit of shopping," she said as she pulled out a large super-charged thermos that kept things frozen for hours. Keturo's eyes grew huge, as did the other children's gathering below, because children have an additional sense for sweets. "Take Suzie and Jared with you, too," she said, motioning to her sister's kids who were kicking a soccer ball.

The children quickly moved out of listening range, though their yelling and laughter faded slowly.

Kendi said, "Y *que*?"

"That's all I know."

"I wonder why they're willing to risk coming here, so close to the village. Did you hear anything about Lucero and his *assasinos*?" Lucero was the region's main drug trafficker, and he hadn't been happy with the direction of the indigenous people. He had stolen much of their land and caused constant conflict. Some of the locals wanted a share of the income from moving the drugs, and the others who wanted Lucero gone struck out on their own. Gunfire had been exchanged, and someone had been shot. Lucero's traffickers had falsely blamed Orlin and Jaora.

"What did you hear at the meeting?"

"We'll vote to become autonomous, I believe, and that will make Lucero even more dangerous. He'll manipulate the malcontents even more."

"Maybe that's why Orlin and Jaora are coming back, to make sure the voting has no interference. And to protect you."

"I want to see Orlin, but I wish he'd stay away until this calms down. The politics and conflict are driving me crazy! I'm not sure who fusses more, the guaras or the humans! How are the guaras doing?"

"The last seven rescued chicks passed their health and flight checks this morning. And now that you're here, we can do the release tomorrow," said Yessenia as she picked up a wayward onion from the wood floor.

"Only seven chicks this year. When we were kids, there were at least fifty every season," Kendi said as took the onion from Yessenia and peeled it.

"We haven't had a poached nest in over five years since the two biggest poachers fell and died. I wouldn't wish that on anyone."

"I wouldn't either, but there are more parrots now. The *rahwa* parrot roost at the river must have had over 300 birds. Those yellow-naped amazon parrots are almost as loud as the macaws, at least that close. Even at the meeting with a microphone we could barely hear each other when the parrots came in for the night."

"Though our seven macaw chicks came to us from natural threats, two flooded cavities and the rest from the April wildfire in sector three, we are still getting birds because of humans. I don't know how we can keep building cages for all the donated birds that take years sometimes to get ready for release. People don't want them for pets anymore."

"I'd like to think that our Apu Pauni project turned everyone around. Papa would be so proud," Kendi said as she wiped her eyes tearing from the onion and her loss.

"Maybe we can take some credit for it from our work with Solidaridad Incondicional. The SI! campaign has positively impacted indigenous and wildlife efforts all over the world."

"That and the suspicion that wild animals carry disease, even parrots!"

Yessenia said, "Listen to us talking to each other like we are leading a parrot consciousness raising meeting. Must mean it's time to remember that life isn't all about parrots. I need to get home to fix dinner and check in on the Saliwas family. They got hit hard this year with Zika and Dengue."

"Every year these insect-transmitted diseases are worse, and new ones are infecting us all the time. I will pray for the family tonight."

"See you tomorrow for the liberation."

Kendi cooked, alternating between the wood fire and gas stove to prepare the pancakes and *wabul*. She thought it was strange that she finally had some quiet, but the quiet made her sad. The kitchen should have been full of relatives cooking, talking, and waiting their turn to eat. But after her mama and papa died, life faded from the house. Her parents had been a force in the community, leading the way with the Apu Pauni project, and building the Lapatista movement based on their slogan, "None Are Free Until All Are Free," that spread throughout the region. Lapatista communities were in nearly every country in the Americas, and she had visited many of them. She and the local villages were well known in the SI! Revolution, that the Lapatistas had merged with. Little did they realize, she thought as she set hot dishes on the table, that the parrots and the preservation movements all hung by a thread. In her darkest moments, that thread became a noose.

As if sensing her thoughts, Rak and two fledglings flew to her porch railing. Kendi smiled. "Thank you for bringing your babies to meet me." The two youngsters with their dark eyes and shorter tails sat quietly, unused to humans. They had hatched in a wild nest, and were not part of the liberation project. Overhead flew an adult macaw keeping watch.

"The whole family out for an evening flight. Would you like something to eat?"

The fledglings eyed the plates of food. As the male leaned in to fly to the table, his sister nipped his ankle. This started a tousling of feet raised and wings stretched. At that same time a crowd of wet children bounded up the stairs, and her sister Mirna followed.

"What's for dinner, Mama?"

"*Naksa, Tia*," multiple children voices called as they jostled for an opening at the table.

Going from peace to chaos in under a minute, the clamoring family signified for Kendi that all was right with the world, even when it wasn't.

"Who would like to say a blessing?"

That silenced everyone as heads hung. From a tree, Rak's mate called with whistles and chortles, and some human sounds that might have been Miskitu, English, or Spanish. Kendi watched the last light fall around the village. Though the red feathers in the trees were turning dark, the humans knew that at dawn the bright red and yellow would fly with the coming sun, an eternal sign that beauty was always present, even when it wasn't obvious.

"I don't know what he just said, but it sounded like a prayer to me," said Kendi.

"Amen" said Lapta.

"Amen, amen, amen," sang out a chorus from Kendi's house, down the path to nearby homes, with solemnity and with joy. The web of life was as abundant as the platters passed around the table, from which feathered and nonfeathered faces ate with delight.

Chapter 11
La Moskitia, Honduras

After sharing the meal, the guara family flew with other macaws into the nearby forest patch. It was dark to be flying, but the fledglings were strong because that's all they'd done all day for three months: fly, chew, fuss with one another, repeat. They were younger than most of this year's fledglings because Rak's first clutch of the family-flower time when eggs are laid and chicks are raised had been lost. She didn't know why her dear eggs hadn't hatched. She'd loved each one of the four and cuddled and covered them for over one white-nut cycle, the waning moon echoing her fading hope. Finally, she couldn't ask Cherk to keep looking for food for both of them if the eggs had died. It wasn't fair. One day she covered them with the small pine chips she and Cherk had painstakingly chewed into soft bits in preparation for the chicks that would never hatch. Cherk brought flowers from the forest patch and laid them over the darkened eggs, and they flew to one of their other home nests. All through that first night, Cherk had preened her softly and uttered soft clucks so that when the sun rose, she flew down from the roost and looked into their second home cavity, which looked fine to her, and then over at Cherk who looked fine too.

The result was these two wonderful children.

Rak's usually fluffed head feathers upon landing were sleek from worry, but not for her chicks or her lost eggs. Her tense mood didn't escape Cherk's notice. It was night, their quiet time; he would ask her at yellow-nut's rising tomorrow. He moved to her side as did the two youngsters, Chret and Reta, who were almost asleep, their crops full of the dinner at Ken Ken's, how Rak referred to Kendi, an endearment derived from the sound a hungry young chick makes. All the macaws now called her Ken Ken. Rak once told Cherk that there had been an older human mother who cared for her when she was young, but she was buried with flowers and dirt, like their eggs.

Cherk understood Rak's admiration for the family who had saved Rak, but he had misgivings. He wanted Chret and Reta to be strong, and worried about their frequent visits to the guardian roosting area. But he couldn't deny them that sweet, cool food that Ken Ken spooned onto the porch railing for his brood. It was the perfect ending for a long day of teaching his children to forage. Before he closed his eyes, he turned his head to make sure the appointed sentinel was high in the trees watching over them all. He turned toward his family, as content as he'd ever been.

Several hours later, the mostly eaten white-nut was now visible through the lower branches, and Rak was more fully awake. Yellow-nut would be rising soon, and Rak fluffed her head feathers in pleasure. She always enjoyed the long relaxing mornings, made even longer with her study of the small white flowers sprinkled over the dark night sky. She could tell that the time of family flower was coming fast and that soon this roosting flock would disperse to their home nests. In fact, some had already gone. She and Cherk had decided not to try this year because Chret and Reta had hatched late and still needed time to learn and grow.

Cherk woke and moved silently farther out on the branch towards Rak to fluff his feathers before he began preening, until Rak made open-beak fake lunges at him.

"Rak, what sits cold in your crop this morning? You didn't seem happy last night either."

"I don't know, but I can tell by the way Ken Ken is acting that something's wrong. I don't want to lose her. I lost Rosa already, and I couldn't bear life without Ken Ken."

"Is no-talking time over?" asked Reta. "What's wrong? Are we safe?"

"Remember the morning rules," said Cherk, lifting his foot and gently placing it back on the branch. "Don't move until you look all around and up." Lifting his foot again, he said, "Look for the sentinel above you. Do they look alert and have they given you the all-is-well signal with their feathers?" Raising his foot again, he said, "Don't fly until yellow-nut lightens your heart and the day. Take time to prepare yourself mentally and physically for the day. Only speak when all this is accomplished."

Both children hung their heads, forgetting once more the routine. Rak and Cherk looked at each other, recalling that all their children were impulsive, as were they in their youth. Wings were meant for flying strong, and beaks for thundering out one's assertion of life, and the young among them were often too quick to take wing and call.

The family preened themselves and each other until Reta asked, "May we hear a story about Rosa?"

Cherk nodded to Rak. The children were old enough now.

"I'll give you Rosa this morning, so you'll carry her with you wherever you fly. The telling and listening are heavy. But I'm going to tell you so you don't carry the burden of what life is, but you fly lighter in gratitude."

"I first knew Rosa when we were both eggs. I could feel her moving next to me, as I could feel Mama's cuddling and hear her soft coos to us. There had been a third sibling, but he died before his eyes opened to see the sweet grandeur of our nest. Rosa was the first to shed her shell and, several yellow-nut cycles later, the first to open her eyes. She was my older sister, and I followed her example when I could. This is not to say that we didn't argue, especially in the heat of the day or when Papa and Mama were late returning to the nest, but she was always with me to give warmth, to preen, and to play.

One day, when we were beginning to see the red in our wings that would one day let us fly over forest and savanna, Mama and Papa were gone, looking for food. Rosa perked up her head, listening hard. I followed her example and heard it, too. Strange sounds came from below our nest, and we followed the nest rule. And what is that?"

"When in the nest alone without parents, remain quiet, especially if you hear anything that is not Mama or Papa," answered Chret, hoping to make them proud of him after he had messed up the awaking routine.

"Good. But I broke the rule because suddenly a loud noise boomed, and the nest floor vibrated. I cried out in fear before Rosa could flap sharply at me. A long silence followed, and I thought we were safe. Sharp sounds broke that hope as the tree shook. I pushed against Rosa, and she covered me with her wings. We heard Mama and Papa giving angry and fearful calls we'd never heard before. I will not repeat them here, for my great wish is that you never have to hear these words, or say them. These are calls that mean the end of life is at hand, and your flock would die for you.

The tree shook fiercely, and then my world ended as the tree fell. I couldn't hold on to Rosa as I was thrown every which way and then out the cavity. The last thing I heard were Mama and Papa crying, and a darkness without white flowers covered me.

I had a dream I was flying, and Rosa was wing-to-wing with me. But I awoke to Rosa grunting, both of us bound up in rough darkness. We were moving, but I couldn't see. I didn't know what to do. Were the nest-time rules broken? I wanted to call out for Mama and Papa, and cry out my fear. But I knew there was a reason for no-talking at night and for the nest quiet rule.

Rosa grew quiet. The heat and stress forced us both to open-beak breathe. Then, suddenly, motion stopped. Some creature grabbed Rosa, who gave such a call of desperation that when that hunter came for me, I attacked, biting as hard as my soft beak could. I heard a cackling sound, like that of the no-flying bird-kind around Ken Ken's roosting home, and again was hurled through the air and landed near Rosa lying on her side. We were finally outside our nest, like we had long talked about, but it wasn't supposed to be like this. Our first time out of nest-home we were supposed to fly, touch each other's wings, but the way Rosa's wings flopped loosely, I didn't know if she would ever fly.

"Mama, who were the hunters?" asked Chret. "Were they eagles? A big snake? A monkey?"

Rak breathed deep and said, "No. They were a kind of guardian."

"But guardians are our friends. They take care of us so that we can fly free. They are liberators."

Cherk remained quiet because he knew this was Rak's story. He had heard the story and had even rubbed beaks with Rosa when he was much younger, before he and Rak became nest-mates.

"Not all of them, children. Some are captors, hunters. These were that kind that stole Rosa and me from the only home we knew."

"But why?"

Rak knew that once she started answering why questions she would never finish the story that must be told for her children to know who they were and where they came from. She also wanted them to understand the liberation ritual that would happen that morning. "Let me finish the telling. You will have your whole lives to learn about such things. Mama had told me about hunters, but she had not told me how big they are. They walk on two legs like we do, but instead of wings, they had snakes."

"Oh Mama, those are hands that can do such wonderful things, like give us great food and even build their own roost-homes," said Reta.

"Those hands can also be cruel. One hunter forced open our beaks to push in the black and white food common among our guardians. They call it *risbean*. Later I learned to like it, but all I wanted to do was to bite the hunter. Rosa choked on the food because she had no strength to swallow. The snake-hand hunters pushed us into their walking fake-nest. We were bound, and the hot swaying began again.

After a long while, the white-nut began to fade and the air

grew darker and cooler. The snake-hand hunters took us out of the fake-nest and forced us to eat. Then they put us back in the fake nest, not binding us, but closing us in. I couldn't see Rosa, but I could tell she was hurt. I wrapped my wings around her to keep us warm, sleeping very little that night or the next after long walks and hot swaying.

On the third day, the hunters were suddenly quiet, and then they ran and threw us through the air, but it didn't cause any more injury. Then all was quiet. Snake-hands reached in to pull us out. I saw them shaking their heads and talking softly. This was my first meeting with guardians. They had chased away the hunters. The guardians took us back to their roost-home. Ken Ken's mama placed us in a wide-open soft fake-nest and we slept and ate in their roost-home, which was warm at night and safe.

Rosa never quit crying. I learned that not only had both her wings been broken in the fall, but so had both her legs. She couldn't stand and ate very little. While my feathers grew out sleek and my wings strong, Rosa had broken feathers, couldn't breathe well, and could only pull herself by her beak to move along the roost-home floors and branches. While I could play with Ken Ken, Rosa kept to herself.

But Rosa wasn't soft. Others would have died or turned hard. Rosa instead grew into a Mama Guara of the roost home. A special guardian came once and gave special flower juice to make Rosa better, but I think it was her will that temporarily won over her disease and pain. For three years she welcomed and protected all new macaws that came to the roost-home before they were strong enough to fly. Though Rosa could never fly, she made it possible for many others to do so. She was almost always with Ken Ken's mother, Apunani, who with Rosa was one of the first two Mama Guaras. When she wasn't with Apunani and Ken Ken, her calm presence in the liberation cage soothed the fear and anger of the many refugees who passed through there on their way to freedom.

"But what happened to Rosa? Did the snake hands come and steal her away again?" Chret and Reta asked.

"Though she was strong in spirit, her body had been weakened. There came a killing cough in the time when the sky-turns-to-river. She became gravely ill. I stayed with her, as did Ken Ken and her mother. The three of us cared for her until her last breath, when she looked at us with wisdom born of suffering and whispered, "*Pree palisa.*"

"I hear the Guardians say this all the time," said Reta.

"Me, too," said Chret. "It means to fly free, doesn't it?"

"Yes, it does. You'll hear it a lot this morning during the liberation. Those seven young ones we've been visiting are going to have their first chance outside the training area. Let's go find our first meal and return strong so we can watch over the young ones. They may be a few white-nut journeys older than you, but they need your wild wisdom and strength. Will you help them, as Rosa would?"

"I will," said Reta. "I want to grow up to be a Mama Guara."

"Me, too," said Chret.

"But Mama, there can only be one, right?" Reta cocked her head.

"You both can be, but you have to learn to work well together, which means flying well," said Cherk. "So, let's begin this morning's lesson by flying wing-to-wing to the sweet, small, green food tree we visited yesterday. Can you find your way there?"

"Not only can I do that, I will get there first!" exclaimed Reta as she jumped off the branch, followed by Chret.

"Wing-to-wing!" cried Cherk who kept his eye on them until they landed, almost at the same time, in the food-tree only fifty wing beats away.

Rak took this rare alone time to tell Cherk, "We must help Ken Ken and the guardians."

"Why? Do you think they're in danger?"

"You've seen the snake-hands gathering in the forest. I believe they mean to destroy the guardian roost homes, just as they did Rosa's and mine, and those of our lost green kin."

"What can we do?"

"I don't know. Without the guardians, we would have disappeared like our green kin. We must help them."

Both children were hanging upside down in the food tree, taking turns letting go, falling, only to fly back to the tree and do it again.

"It's hard to be aware that there is such harm in a world of such joy," said Rak heavily, bowing her head as Cherk reached over to soothe her with preening.

"That's it!" Rak said suddenly, her feathers sleek and head high. "We must celebrate and spread joy, even in the midst of harm. It's our turn to give back to the guardians. Let's gather our kind and kin to show our thanks. Maybe we'll hatch new wisdom about what else can be done."

"Let's do this. I'll fly far and spread the call to wings."

"I'll fly as far as the children can and do the same."

Just then, automatic rifle shots tore through the northern forest patch.

"Let's go. The danger is happening!" cried Cherk.

They raised their wings, then one foot and the other and jumped into the air, Cherk headed toward the snake-hand ground thunder, but made a circle around the source and dodged the many startled birds in the air.

"Flee, flee!" cried the smaller birds.

"Fly free!" Cherk boomed over their voices. He could be heard far and wide.

The humans below were yelling similar sentiments. Torn between fleeing and freeing, they grabbed their phones so their story would be known, no matter how it ended.

Chapter 12
South Australia

Nikau entered the isolation suite, embarrassed to walk in on Jule changing into, in fact, pajamas.

"Sorry, I should've knocked."

"Hey, don't worry. We're now pandemic pals," said Jule smiling.

Aria and Nikau both groaned at once as their eyes fixed on Jule's shoulder tattoo. The bright yellow and red feathers and the long tail that reached half way to her elbow clearly identified it as a scarlet macaw, and the bird's foot raised in the air along with the bold letters SI! under it marked Jule as a member of the Lapatista movement. They both stepped closer to admire her tattoo, Aria tracing her finger along the raised macaw's wings.

"I didn't know you were part of SI! And a Lapatista as well. When did you join?"

"Just a few weeks ago. The last little scab fell off last week. I'd wanted to be part of the movement for years but was afraid what it might mean to my career. You said the vows last night, Aria, but did you consider joining?"

Aria looked at Nikau who nodded in agreement. They took off their shirts that covered large, transparent bandages on their right shoulders.

Jule stepped over to Aria, "You got a kea. And you, Nikau?"

"A kea as well. We barely had time to get them before the conference."

Jule said, "I hate to be the odd one out," and took out her phone. She made a few swipes and stabs at it. To their amazement, the bright colors of the scarlet macaw faded into the muted colors of a kea.

"Oh, a smart tattoo!"

"I don't know how smart it is. The technology really hasn't been proven. I might just get *beschissen* if it gets a bug in it and my last blurry selfie will be branded on my shoulder for life.

"That didn't take long. We're thirty minutes into lockdown, and we've all already taken off our shirts," Aria said glancing at her phone. Pulling her shirt back on, she said "I've got to go. My presentation starts in a few minutes."

She walked into her cubby-room and shut the door, as did the other two. Jule wanted to keep her pajamas on, and thought about projecting one of her avatars in her place, but Aria might appreciate seeing her real face in the crowd.

Jule was putting on her conference clothes when Aria began her presentation, "Perfect Pathogens in Parrots," to an emptier room than expected. She was glad to see Jule walk in, while people chuckled about not only her constant alliterations but her visuals. She even earned a gasp when she had a feathered velociraptor spring into the room hunting to make the point how the origins of some of the pathogens developed eons ago, possibly back when birds were still theropod dinosaurs. Toward the end of the talk, her phone vibrated several times, the pattern alerting her to a message from New Zealand. She rushed through the last part of her talk, and as she reached for her phone Helga's holo walked to the front of the virtual room and said, "Thank you, Dr. Ropata, that was a perfectly pertinent presentation. We'll now take questions. Raise your hand either as a holo-person or in the chat room."

Several hands went up. Aria was about to tell Helga that she would take questions after the next talk when she heard, "Yes, Dr. Luther Jennings."

He said, "Thank you, Dr. Ropata, for a wonderful presentation. I was particularly interested in the presence of prions in parrots. Have you ever seen any indication that a prion disease can be passed from birds to humans?"

"No, it's never been documented. Avian prions have a particular structure and don't interact with mammal biological systems and vice versa."

"But have any avian prions been found in humans, whether causing disease or not?"

"Again, not that I know of. But we haven't really looked because there has been no zoonotic disease to trigger an investigation."

"Yes, Dr. Vogel?" Helga responded to Jule's raised hand.

Jule said, "We've just begun a study of the presence of avian prions in various kinds of environmental samples, such as soil, crops, pastures, and intensive animal agriculture substrates, which could lead us to looking at their presence in human biosystems. But, so far, we're just collecting samples and doing rudimentary analysis."

"Thank you, Dr. Vogel and Dr. Ropata," said Luther. "I have many more questions. Will you please message me so I don't take up any more conference time?"

Jule and Aria quickly set their conference communication settings to accept private messages from Luther, wondering if this had to do with Isaac's condition. They holoed-out of the next presentation to find out. They each left their single rooms to meet in the community space of their isolation suite.

"Room, call Luther Jennings, volume low." Aria didn't want to disturb Nikau's conference group during the 2-way call. Luther's image jumped up on the room projection system in 2D.

"Hello, Aria and Dr. Vogel," greeted Luther.

"Call me Jule."

"And I'm Luther. I'm so glad you called right away. I need help from both of you. First, let me say that Isaac is doing fine, though we haven't figured out what is going on with him. We still can't identify the prion that is in his system, and there doesn't seem to be a genetic cause, but we'll know for sure when we analyze your family's genetics."

Aria breathed a sigh of relief, for herself and for so many she loved.

"So, what can we do? We are under lockdown at the conference because of Isaac," said Aria.

"Sorry about that, but we felt it was necessary as we don't know what we are dealing with. And that's where you can help me think this through. You see, we did a retrospective study of people showing similar symptoms. We then sent them or their surviving family and friends alerts and surveys to fill out. They are under home quarantine as well, though with a slow acting prion disease that is acquired through ingestion and is not transmitted through air or contact, it's not really necessary. However, I don't have to tell you, better safe than sorry, and all that. Not to mention health-care politics."

"I still don't understand how we can help," Aria interrupted, urging Luther to cut to the chase.

"One of the set of questions that the survey asks is about contact with animals, especially wild animals."

"Yes, we know. That's standard. What did you find?" asked Aria. Jule was content to let Aria lead the communication.

"The AI is still sifting through the surveys, and we've broadened our case study to include large samples of New Zealand's population. It's going to take a while to weed out the interference, but we did get a couple of cases where people who died with symptoms had contact with birds, and, more intriguing, with parrots. Even though it's a long shot that birds could be implicated, we'd like to get a head start on this."

"What do you want us to do?"

"I'd like to see if the prion in Isaac, and maybe others we'll take samples from, is of avian origin."

Aria stalled, saying, "But all my avian prion substrates and gear are in my lab in Christchurch, and Isaac's sample is there too. And I'm stuck here."

"Wait a minute. Some of your samples are here for our environmental studies project," said Jule.

"And I can send some of Isaac's samples by speed-drone, which should get to you by tonight," said Luther.

"All we need is a lab where we can process samples the long way, with the older standard ELISA methodology. After that we can worry about calibrating a PCMA reader, if we need to."

"Maybe we can use the Adelaide Infectious Disease Laboratory," Jule said, already working out the details. "They are set up for housing staff during outbreaks on site, and since Australia is still marked green, except for our hotel that's in orange, we can move there. It's across town."

"I really hate to ask you to do all this because it might not be anything yet. It might be an aberration in Isaac," said Luther. "But I think you have a better chance of working this out with your expertise there instead of me working with scientists in New Zealand who are unfamiliar with avian prions."

"We're happy to help. And if this all blows over, I can be back in New Zealand in a few days and continue there," said Aria, whose fingers were already itching to start making the arrangements.

"That's great. I've sent you links so you can join our Communicable Diseases Investigation Team (CDIT) to get the latest results and be part of all meetings and decisions, as this perhaps nonevent fizzles out. And remember, this is confidential. Rumors might cause more harm than any actual disease."

"Okay. See you in the cloud," said Aria.

"Kia ora," said Luther.

Luther's live video had not faded before both Jule and Aria were sending messages. The first was a private message to Helga, who winked out her holo in the current presentation and called Aria.

"What's up, Aria?"

"We need to keep this confidential. The CDIT has asked us to see if the samples from my uncle could be of avian origin. We're going to need the IDL lab and probably extra lab equipment. Can you help us?

"And if anyone asks what's going on?"

"Tell them it's a drill."

"That might work, though I already denied it was a drill. Send me a list of what you and Jule need. I better get back to the presentation."

Aria and Jule decided to not holo-in to the current presentation because it would be obvious they weren't paying attention as they made calls and packed up. They did connect to the live video stream of the current presenter who, unfortunately, was having to compete with several people distracted by what they thought was a drill and were checking MASCD alerts.

"We should be able to get started after dinner. The samples from New Zealand will arrive by then, along with the equipment," said Aria.

"Should we attend the conference? It's almost lunch time, then the discussion on trends, and then there will be roundtables in the evening. But we don't have to decide now."

"Speaking of lunch, I'm starved," said Nikau exiting his room. "Hey what's going on?" he said eyeing their travel bags. "Did the quarantine break already?"

Aria felt her face flush. She'd forgotten about telling Nikau what was going on.

"Luther wants us to work on investigating if Isaac's sample will react with my kea samples and Jule's avian prion samples. We have to move into the IDL."

A long silence stretched as Nikau resisted a pout.

"Just the two of you are leaving?"

Aria took his hands. "Ah, Nikau, I don't want to pull you away from the conference and possibly expose you to any more disease. It's going to be a lot of indoor, intense lab work with little sleep."

Nikau said, "Okay, first, I think the conference is a bust, and I can attend wherever I am, either here in the isolation suite or from the lab. Two, the lab is surely set up to protect any of the workers from disease, and I can help, a lot. I might not know how to process prion samples, but I'm a lab rat from way back. And, finally, I wasn't planning on sleeping much during the conference anyway."

Aria's face flushed even more. Jule waited for them to work it out.

He said, "Come on, in for a penny, in for a pound, and all that rot."

Aria looked at Jule who nodded. Aria said, "Okay then. Let's make it a portable pajama party!"

Jule and Nikau groaned, just as lunch was delivered in the entry room. Aria and Jule caught Nikau up on the details while the room projection system surrounded them with an ocean seascape of the islands near Adelaide. Intermixed with their conversation were little penguins chirping and croaking on the beaches and in the rocks. Nikau said he heard from his uncle who said they had no suspects in the kea disappearances. "No Kiwi kidnapping!" Nikau challenged them.

"Just keas in cahoots," braved Jule.

Aria pretended to ignore them in favor of the scenery. "I sure hope we go there after the conference," she said, jumping up and twirling around as she ran her fingers through the holo island scene. She stumbled on the last turn and fell into Nikau's arms, who then pretended to fall, taking Jule with them onto a sofa.

He said, "It looks like we are having a Pile-on Picnic!"

"Or maybe a kinky k-not," Aria eked out, as if she'd been saving it for their word game.

Giggles erupted, faded, and then cycled around again. No

one was quick to untangle, listening instead to the waves and the penguins and each other's heart beats.

"I'm going to check in on our avian intelligence conference while I'm packing," Nikau said without moving.

"How's that going?" asked Aria.

That got Nikau moving. He said, "We're pretty sure that there are statistically significant increases in the II in the kea population, not just in New Zealand, but around the world. Now we're trying to find out why and how this is possible. Pathologists and geneticists are presenting this afternoon, followed by roundtables on the results, including the recent tapes and events with the New Zealand wild flock. I can plug in on the ride to the lab and at the lab. Speaking of which, I better go pack."

Aria and Jule slouched on the couch, delaying calling a car a little longer. They got up only when their bio-personal protective equipment (Bio-PPE) was delivered. Nikau joined them, and all three covered themselves, sprayed down their bags, then stepped into the hallway, hoping to leave without being seen. Instead, the hall was lined with conference attendees who clapped and cheered.

Nikau whispered, "This is how it plays out in movies right before the heroes start dropping, one by one."

When they passed Helga, she shrugged and said, "They're too smart. They knew what was happening. The avian disease conference is at your service when you need us."

"Yes," said Dr. Mbungo. "I have a lot of experience with parrot neural physiology and disease, and if you can use an extra pair of hands, I'm available."

Several others nearby nodded in agreement.

Aria said, "We'll let you know. Let's get the IDL set up, and the first batch of samples going. In the meantime, please continue with the conference, and we'll holo-in from the lab." She patted her heart in thanks and turned to the waiting car.

At the lab they threw their bags into their isolation suite and entered the special isolation wing of the lab to double-check the equipment. They were met by the lab director, Dr. Daku Williams, who had cleared bench space for them.

"I'm sorry I can't give you a full tour of the place. We need to restrict your movements so you work as far from everyone else as possible. I understand that you are working with prions, which have never been confirmed to be airborne or contact transmitted, but let's be cautious."

"Thanks for giving us the space on such short notice," Aria offered, and the others nodded.

"That's what we're here for. If you need anything, just ask for me through the room communication and projection system. Their name is Bob," said Dr. Williams as he disappeared through a door.

The three were too busy to focus on the conference meetings, even with Bob projecting on every wall and the ceiling. They had to do preparatory lab work and check results on the CDIT cloud system. Aria called Isaac and her mom to see how they and Callum were doing. Donika reported that since the family was under home quarantine, the diagnostic team had gone to the house to perform a spinal tap on Callum and take other samples. Donika said she and the volunteers continued looking for the keas, on horseback and in the ATV.

"But no sign of any keas, either the wild flock or the escapees. Nada."

"Nikau's uncle told him that there were no signs of human

involvement."

"I wonder what they're up to. We've never seen anything like this."

"I'll call again tonight. Got to get back to the conference."

"Kia ora."

"Kia ora."

Aria wanted to tell her mom about their lab project, but she didn't want to be the source of any rumors that might explode out of Kowhai Ranch if the volunteers got wind of it. She had checked her MASCD right before calling, and the nonconfirmed social overlay showed New Zealand turning from darker shades of yellow to orange, though the official status was pinpoints of red where people were under home quarantine. As the number of surveys that were requested and returned mounted, people knew something was up.

By dinner, the equipment and supplies had arrived. Jule and Aria started processing Isaac's sample by first incubating it and making sure they had plenty of prion to work with. This would take several hours. While they waited, they sorted Jule's samples so they could quickly test the incubated solution against a large array of known prions, using prion antibodies that had been engineered against prion proteins.

Nikau, fascinated with all things scientific, hovered around. "You have to incubate Isaac's sample first?"

"That's right, to get lots of the target prion protein that's in his system," said Aria.

"What's the ultrasound equipment for?"

"To blast the prions into smaller parts, making even more prion protein fragments available."

"What's Jule doing?"

"She's preparing the ELISA plates that we'll fill with Isaac's prion. That will attach to solutions we pour over them to see if his prion is a match with any others. The plates take a couple of hours to saturate."

"And what are you doing?"

"I'm mixing up the solution for each prion protein that we'll pour onto the ELISA plates."

"How many different prion proteins are you going to test for?"

"We'll start at the beginning, just to double check Luther's work, looking for BSE and some other mammal spongiform encephalopathy prion diseases, and then move on to the collection of wildlife we have, beginning with birds."

"What –"

Aria said, "Would you like to help Jules prepare the plates or help me make the solutions?"

"Oh sure. Bob, split screens with a one-way using the disease conference link and with the avian intelligence conference link. Broadcast the avian intelligence audio to my personal communication system." Nikau wanted to make sure that people couldn't see what they were doing, to diffuse the rumor mill. They worked in outward silence until Luther's emergency call overran the room system. His frowning continence shown through the technology quite clearly.

"Any results yet?" he asked with zero preamble.

"No, we still have an hour or more before we can run the first test. How's it going on your end?"

"Have you checked MASCD recently? The nonconfirmed social overlay has gone nuts, as have our survey results. More people are reporting they have loss of balance, trouble walking and talking, and are acting crazy. The cloud also blew up with talk of Zealand Zombie Disease after a video was posted of a woman having a psychic break or hallucination and chasing after people in Christchurch, but not very well because she had poor balance. The police are looking for her now on the off chance that she's connected to Isaac's case. We need to know not only what Isaac has, but if others have it as well. I'm rushing spinal and blood samples to you, from your grandfather and a few others. We're also putting a rush on some pathology samples from those who died with the most suspicious symptoms. Let me know as soon as you know anything."

In the background they heard a crash and a scream, then Luther jumped and spun away. "Bloody hell!" he yelled before running off. The screen blanked.

They froze in stunned silence a moment before all three hurriedly opened their phones.

"I gotta call Mom!" Aria squeaked.

"I'll try to call Luther back and see what happened. Maybe it's not what we're thinking," said Jule. "Bob, project MASCD results on screen."

There, filling the whole room, was New Zealand flashing red, like a beating heart ripped out of a chest.

Chapter 13
Southern Australia

"Aria, I'm glad you called," said Donika.

"Is everything okay?"

"Yes, we're fine here. I didn't call because I didn't want you to worry."

"Why? What's happening? We've been pretty isolated and distracted with a conference project."

"Christopher showed me a video of a woman going loco in Christchurch, and with a few households under quarantine, the conspiracy theories and fake news reports are surging. Zombies, indeed!"

"I'm glad you're okay, Mom." Aria sucked in a deep breath. "We are, too."

"What's wrong? I know when you aren't telling me something."

Aria took a deeper breath. Her news was no worse. "Isaac's doctor, Luther Jennings, asked me to work on some samples because there might be a connection to the keas. Jule, Nikau, and I left the conference to work at the IDL in Adelaide. We'll run samples through the night and tomorrow."

"It looks like I'll be up all night, too. Callum is having a bad spell that eases when I'm in the room."

"Thanks, Mom, for taking care of him. Let's talk again in the morning."

"And thank you for taking care of Isaac by researching his disease."

"Kia ora."

"Kia ora."

Aria glanced at Jule who was getting off the phone.

Jule said, "I couldn't reach Luther, but the CDIT postings said they have a new patient acting like the woman in the video, except she smashed up the E.R. before they could subdue her."

"Bob, connect visual to my phone," Nikau said. He swiped away from the image of throbbing red New Zealand to surf through the associated stats and news reports keyed to the map. The room felt like a police car had crashed with flashing lights.

"Turn off the 3D and turn down the sound!" Aria cried. The room was quiet.

Nikau sat on a lab stool. "Look, guys, the CDIT just posted the survey results. The correlation to those showing the most extreme symptoms with, wow, not just any birds, but with parrots, has increased slightly. And more patients have some kind of prion in their cerebrospinal fluid."

All their devices and Bob flashed a red alert, announcing the closing of New Zealand to international travel and restricting in-country movement.

"This conference sure isn't going like I thought it would," said Nikau. "But I'm not here for a pity party," he said, his attempt at humor. "Tell me how to do everything. The sooner we figure this out, the sooner we can get back to normal."

Though they'd been children during the Corona and Flu

Years, they knew that sometimes disease outbreaks turned into smoldering pandemics that never disappeared. With that in mind, they turned to their work until, an hour later, Helga called offering further assistance. Aria said they were okay for now, but depending how the first wave of results turned out they might need her later. "In fact, I'll add you to the CDIT so you can add the names of people who could help. Thanks," Aria said and hung up.

Jule said, "I have 20 plates prepared and more in process. Which do we run first?"

"Let's start with a control plate for every PrP we test for, just to double-check the row of controls on each ELISA plate. Then let's run the known prion proteins that cause disease, like our BSE and PrPSC solutions, and then our domestic birds, the chicken, turkey, duck, and goose prions, and then a bird from each Order," she said, looking over the many labeled solutions, "A penguin, a hawk." She listed several more, finishing with, "And then our parrots, a kea from New Zealand, a wild budgerigar, a cockatiel, a galah from Australia, and a homed budgerigar and cockatiel from New Zealand. That should do it."

"PrP, that's Prion Protein, right?" Nikau asked. "And what's PrPSC?"

"That's sheep scrapie, and the BSE is Bovine Spongiform Encephalopathy."

"Both are prion diseases. The first doesn't infect humans, but the second does," Jule added.

Nikau watched them fill the plates. When they were done, he asked, "What now?"

Jule said, "We wait two hours, wash the plates, then add the colorimetric substrate."

"So, we're going to need some prion patience," he said.

"Which will be easier to come by," said Aria, "because our piping hot pizza just arrived."

Jule said, "And I asked Daku to pick us up some Little Creature Pale Ale, which should be chilling in our shared space."

Aria said, "Let's get out of our bio-PPE and go relax. As my old professor used to say, a watched ELISA plate never finishes."

They sat down to eat, and Aria told Bob to show the night sky on all the lab and dormitory screens. They could see the main lab through the transparent walls of their living space. "Play night wave and party music tracks," Aria told Bob.

"I don't know that genre," said Bob. "Would you like something from the Pacific islands, perhaps with ukuleles or didgeridoos?"

"Bob, why don't you surprise us?" Aria suggested.

"Beach Blanket Bingo," blared over the sound system, the first of many of Bob's surprises.

They passed an hour, laughing and almost forgetting the outside world, until Nikau asked, "What do you think we'll find?"

"My guess is that we won't see any color reaction at all. It's too hard to believe we have a new prion disease from birds. Maybe that's wishful thinking on my part because we don't have the science to explain how it could happen," Aria said.

"How much more time?" Nikau asked, finishing his beer.

"Thirty minutes."

They checked their CCs and CDIT messages before they put on their bio-PPE. Aria said, "Bob, allow two-way holo connections to the CDIT group."

The lab room suddenly filled with people who gathered around as the plates were washed and the colorimetric substrate was added, then the stop solution, and then the final wash solution. The three placed each plate in the ELISA reader connected to the room screens. If there was a match of Isaac's prion to any other prions, the colorimetric substrate would adhere to the ELISA plate and register as a color, the darker red the greater the concentration.

Aria said, "That's good the control plate is clear. The BSE wells are also clear, so that confirms Luther's result showing that Isaac doesn't have that disease. Looks like our lab technique was good. Whoops, I spoke too soon, the PrPSC plate is showing a slight positive, invisible to the naked eye but present."

She scrunched her eyes, considering what that meant. "We'll continue on, though I don't know how to explain that result."

They inserted one bird after another, all showing a negative reaction even at the higher concentrations of Isaac's sample. Picking up the kea plate, the collective intake of breath whooshed over the room. The plate was bright red in nearly all wells. The ELISA reader confirmed this, with the controls showing no reaction. Aria focused on the process instead of what it meant by finishing the rest of the parrot samples, some of which showed a low concentration reaction.

"What does it mean?" asked Luther.

"I don't know yet," said Aria.

Helga suggested, "Why don't we take a few minutes to discuss how to interpret this and the next steps, and then come back together in fifteen minutes."

The room erupted in chatter as the group broke off into smaller breakout rooms showing the results of the twenty plates on all screens. Aria and Jule joined the avian disease group, full of avian veterinarians, and mammalian and human prion experts.

Fifteen minutes later, when the small groups merged together, Aria said, "Here's our hypothesis. Luther's prion is definitely a prion from this kea, but we don't know if other keas have the same prion. So, we must test more keas to see if they have the same prion as this kea and Isaac. The other parrots might have a very low concentration of the kea protein, or perhaps there is some cross reactivity as parrot prions are similar to one another. We need to test other parrots, as well as other birds, to see if they have the kea's prion.

"And the reactivity with the sheep prion?" Luther asked the question on everyone's mind.

Aria hesitated to jump to conclusions, but she wasn't the only one who'd considered a true linkage between kea and human, with sheep involved. "Until we run more tests, it seems possible that the prion that causes scrapie shares similar structure to that of this kea, and perhaps we have a mammal-kea transmission that involves sheep, at least one human, and at least one kea."

"But sheep do not have scrapie in New Zealand," said a holo attendee unknown to Aria.

"They don't now, but there have been brief occurrences in the past," volunteered another.

Helga, ever the leader, asked, "So what is the recommendation of this group?"

"Do the tests I suggested, along with the new batch of Luther's samples, which should arrive soon. We'll know more after that," said Aria.

"I can arrange to get more samples from captive keas in Australia and other parrots," said Jule.

"I can do the same with my New Zealand colleagues," said Aria, "but I don't know how many samples we can get. The wild flock and the liberated captive keas have apparently disappeared. But I have samples in my lab. Luther, could you send those as well? They are in isolation orange boxes labeled as kea whole blood, kea plasma, and kea brain/spinal cord. We can also produce enough of the kea protein using PMCA and adapt it so it'll work with any PMCA reader anywhere."

Luther said, "This will take a couple of days to get results. What do we tell people now? And how do we restrict their movements?"

"We know that prion diseases are either genetic or caused by eating parts of cows that have BSE, so we tell people to quit eating kea-lime pie?" a holo pathologist from New Zealand said, attempting humor.

When groans instead of laughs came, Aria jumped in. "We know that in other species' prion diseases, the various spongiform encephalopathies are spread by body fluids or ingestion of contaminated food or forage. So, if you are in the environment of a parrot, or work with parrots, you could be susceptible. I think we need to warn people not to handle keas, isolate from them, and only care for them and their environments with full bio-PPE."

"But there are keas all over the world. They've been poached, sold, and shipped to collections for years and years, with illegal activity still moving them around the world. We need to make a global statement," Jule said.

"This could cause widespread panic and perhaps harm to keas, parrots, and other birds. We don't know how people will react," Aria protested.

"But if we don't say anything now, we could lose more lives and cause more harm." Luther countered.

"So damned either way." Helga said.

"That's always the way with these emerging diseases. I suggest we issue an advisory that we may have a rare occurrence of some agent that may occur in both keas and people, and advise precautions until further notice? Any dissent?" Luther paused. "Further discussion?" Luther asked, warming to leading the CDIT, even though as a referring physician he had no claim on the position. He discovered he admired Helga, and smiled.

"I think the team in this lab is going to need more help. I would like to move to the lab and help," offered Dr. Mbungo.

"But are you sure? We don't know what we are working with or how it's spread," Aria said.

Dr. Mbungo said, "I've worked with parrots all my life and have said I would give my life for them. Here's my chance."

"You'd be most welcome, Baraka," said Jule who had known him for years. "I'll arrange it with the lab."

"Aria and Jule, if you could keep the lab vids open, we'll continue to collaborate as samples and results come in. I'll assign people to work with the model emerging disease AI that we've been building for years. That way your hands and minds can be free for the front-line measures," said Helga.

"So, there will be no goodbye tonight," said Baraka.

"No, but we say *kia ora*, all. Be safe," said Aria.

"Kia ora. Be safe," chimed many voices.

"What are you thinking, Aria?" Jule asked, noticing Aria's sudden faraway look.

"I never thought about it before, but *kia ora* means so many things."

"*Ora* means life, and *kia* puts action into it. It wishes others the essence of life, or as it's come to mean, be safe, be well, or even just hello or goodbye," said Nikau.

"We know," said Aria giving Nikau the hand signal for mansplaining, an "m" formed with curled fingers on both hands touching to make a heart. "But *kia* and kea are pronounced the same way, and *ora* means to pray in Spanish. So –" she said, taking their hands and looking at them, "– I want to wish you and all living beings on Earth kea prayers. I don't know if there is any real risk in what we're doing, or in what we've spent most of our lives doing, but regardless, I'm grateful to be sharing this time with you."

Nikau and Jule both repeated, "*Kea ora*, Aria."

Nikau added, "Is there any beer and pizza left?"

"It's almost morning, I'm switching to coffee," Jule said moving to the break station.

"And lots of it," Aria agreed.

"Make it so, number ones," Nikau commanded, linking with Jule's and Aria's arms.

Aria said, "We are indeed entering an undiscovered country where no one has gone before."

LORAKIM JOYNER

Chapter 14
Kentucky, USA

"Get 'em off me! Get 'em off!" screamed Adonis. He was huddled frozen in a corner of the cage, with a dozen cockatoos hanging on him and flying at his head and eyes. The dark bills probed his coveralls, looking for something more substantial to dig into, while others tested the thickness of his boots. The parrots' screams and bodies with their long out-stretched wings nearly obscured the man and his cries.

Ronnie sensed chaos from the kitchen where he was preparing food for a thousand parrots in the long building. He glanced at the vid screens, confident the new volunteer who was being attacked wouldn't be in any real danger in a head-to-toe protective suit, a crash helmet, and thick gloves and boots, all standard equipment for entering that particular flight of aggressive cockatoos. But Adonis had panicked. Ronnie dropped his knife and said, "Shit, I don't have time for this!" as he took off running as fast as his old legs would go.

He ran past various size cages and flights until he reached the last one, which held the rowdiest and most mentally disturbed cockatoos. Only trained people were allowed to care for them. But Adonis had insisted he was ready, and he seemed to be accepted by the birds, so he'd gone in to clean the perches and add new toys.

By the time Ronnie reached the aviary, all was quiet. Adonis was pressed into the corner with his hands over his eyes, gasping, while the cockatoos were sitting quietly on their perches. A few flew to the front of cage when Ronnie entered the safe room.

"You guys need to quit harassing the volunteers and staff," Ronnie admonished. Two cockatoos raised their white and pink crests, and others lowered them, inviting Ronnie to scratch their heads. He wanted to reach through the aviary wire to touch them, but, one, he was pissed and didn't want to reinforce bad behavior as a ploy to get attention, and, two, it was against sanctuary rules to touch the birds. But they craved touch, so often he and others broke the rules to keep their own hearts from breaking. But not today, not in front of Adonis, if he ever looked up.

"Adonis, it's okay. Come on out. They aren't going to hurt you. Adonis?"

Adonis looked up; his eyes big, afraid to make eye contact with the birds. He didn't want to see their intelligent intent or anger, and he didn't want to trigger another attack. He looked down as he stood, made himself as small as possible and walked to the front of the cage. He passed cockatoos on perches, some staring at him, some screaming, others raising their crests, and some lunging for him without leaving their perches. At the front of the cage, he froze again, afraid to remove his googles for the retinal scanner.

"Adonis, when I open the inner door, step into the safe room quickly. Adonis raised his eyes and nodded. Ronnie leaned his face and centered his eye on the scanner until the inner cage door popped open. Adonis fell into the inner room, slamming the door closed as feathered screaming bodies flew at him, grasped the door, and swung their heads back and forth.

"Do you see that?" shouted Adonis as he put on his usual over-confident smirk to get through his toughest days. "They were all over me! What set them off?"

"We'll review the recordings, but I'm guessing they were playing with you, maybe trying to get my attention. They've done this before, but never so dramatically."

Stepping out into the flight common hallway, Adonis said, "Hell of a way to ask to have your head scratched."

"Like humans, traumatized victims often don't know how to ask, and they act out in detrimental ways to others and themselves. There's no blame or shame to the wounds we all carry for society."

"I thought I had some friends in this flight, but they turned on me," said Adonis, his shoulders slumping. "I also thought volunteering would help heal my PTSD, not trigger it."

Ronnie placed his hand on Adonis's back. "You've got a lot of friends here. Okay? Also, that's the sanctuary's toughest flight of birds and has been for decades. Very few people can work with them or even want to. They are either breaking your heart or your skin, and sometimes both at the same time."

"I really wanted to help out. I know how short-staffed you are."

"That we are, that we are. Speaking of which, why don't you finish in the kitchen and I'll finish here."

Adonis couldn't cover his relief. He said, "Sure, man. I'll leave it to the famous cockatoo whisperer," and walked down the aisle to the kitchen, with his helmet gripped against his chest as if he'd never let it go.

Ronnie turned to the many sets of eyes that had followed their conversation, moods, and words. "What am I going to do with you all?"

He stared into the retinal scanner and entered the aviary after throwing his jacket over the camera lens. He didn't don protective gear.

"I know it's not your fault. You've all been through so much." He made a point of meeting every bird's eyes as he spoke, lingering on Bess's body wrap. "Glad you're leaving that alone, Bess. We don't need you tearing at your chest and bleeding out like last time." Hearing her name, she lowered her head, and Ronnie, without pausing, scratched her head and neck and pulled on her feet.

He heard heavy wing flaps behind him and turned smiling. "Oh hey, Hercules," he said and bowed to the largest bird in the aviary, one of several Moluccan cockatoos. Hercules, in response, bowed his head, but didn't raise his crest. "Something's wrong, isn't it, my man?"

"Scrrreete!" Hercules bellowed and bounced.

"I know this isn't the wild forests of your ancestors, but it's better than that unheated garage I found you in, right?"

Hercules tilted his head and shook it back and forth.

"No? I guess you're right. Prison is prison, no matter how big you build the cage."

At that, Hercules lifted his foot and pounded it on a perch. Several more cockatoos on that row did the same. Ronnie had seen this before. It reminded him of films with prisoners who showed defiance by making rhythmic sounds with their cups, hands, or voices. He started picking up Adonis's tools. Hercules flew to the ground and picked up two rope-block toys with his beak. He walked to Ronnie and dropped them at his feet.

"Thanks, Herc. Where would you like me to put these?"

Hercules turned his head to the farthest reaches of the flight, where a group of silent cockatoos pressed into each other in fear.

"Okay, let's give them the toys. They hardly ever move from that corner."

Hercules and Ronnie chatted as Ronnie finished cleaning up. Several other cockatoos came to watch, picked up tools, and walked or flew back and forth, inviting Ronnie to chase them. It's a game they all enjoyed, but Ronnie wasn't in the mood.

"Sorry I can't play today. I've got a meeting over at the Parakeet Pavilion, like, wow!" he said, looking at his old-fashioned wristwatch, "in five minutes."

He headed toward the door, turned, put his hands together in Namaste fashion and bowed. Many cockatoos bowed their heads, their crests splaying broadly.

"I sure wish I could do that, guys, and so much more. I know you feel like you've been abandoned, hell, most of you were. But I love you and promise your outdoor flight cage will soon be ready. It will not only be repaired, but it's five times bigger. We just gotta get through winter first, okay?"

Ronnie limped back to the kitchen, saw Adonis was okay, and entered the transition room to shower and change clothes. He hated all the rigmarole and missed the days of moving around the sanctuary in shorts and flip flops. But he knew procedures were necessary after several disease outbreaks and with the privilege of the establishment on his Kentucky sanctuary grounds of the headquarters, labs, and flights of prestigious PACT. He loved the acronym and whispered each word as if in prayer, Pochelani

Alliance and Conservation Trust. It was right and good to use the indigenous word instead of the European designation for parakeet, as befitted PACT's origins during the Extinction Rebellion. He was proud of that history that both Eddie and he took part in. The purpose of PACT was to stop extinction and offer reparations for the past and any ongoing harm to life on the planet. The extinct Carolina parakeet was their banner bird, a story that began in beauty, seemed to end in tragedy, but was now in its de-extinguished beauty phase. He couldn't discern where this project was ultimately heading, but at least he saw his work as moving in the right direction, at least most days.

Jumping into the golf cart, he sped to the meeting. Though the sanctuary was doing well, he thought they didn't need to splurge on smart carts. He corrected himself that the sanctuary was doing well in some regards, but not in others. In the foyer of the Parakeet Pavilion, he passed school children gathered around The Cage. The Cincinnati Zoo had donated the relic. Two species had gone extinct in its confines. First, the last passenger pigeon, Martha, and then Inca, the last Carolina parakeet. Holographic projections showed Inca in the cage as the species story was told, and then slowly disappeared, feather by feather until the computer narrator ended with, "It took over 100 years since their deaths for a small group of humans to unite in covenant to end the loss of life on our planet. We emphasized the parrots of the world and promised nevermore and evermore. And so, PACT was born."

He didn't stop to see the children's faces, but he knew what he'd see if he had the time. They would be open-mouthed, some would cry, and the adults would nod their heads in affirmation. Then one green feather would appear in the cage, and the recording would continue after a reflective pause, "And with your help we can bring back the Carolina parakeet and open the cage door. Please donate today to keep parrots flying free." The tour guide would wave her phone in front of the scanner and another green feather would appear along with the loud "Sakreet" call of the Carolina parakeet. The kids would rush to the scanner, squealing with delight as, with each donation, the parakeet took on more form until, to the children's amazement, the holographic door would open and dozens of parakeets would fly out, swirling around the children and up into the domed skylight, where they'd disappear.

As he waited for the elevator, Ronnie could hear the children's joy. He looked to the right at the holo-mirror that was unattended. It still shocked him how old and round he looked, his tanned white face sagging into jowls. He said, "Leadbeater cockatoo," and the mirror transformed his reflection into a beautiful mixture of his human features and those of the cotton-candy striped bird. As he stepped into the elevator, the mirror said, "Let the beauty you are be what you do." He gave a tight smile, dreading the endless meeting ahead of him, and whispered, "Beauty my ass."

As he stepped into the conference room, he saw more than the usual board members and key representatives of their partner affiliates filling the room. Sometimes he tired of the neo-teal method of organizational structure, because so much was happening, he could barely keep track. He was glad to see his main support, Kasuku, chatting with a clump of in-person attendees. Kasuku, who used the pronoun they, was the best vice-president and hence president-elect that PACT had ever had. They always managed to look energetic and refreshed, not like someone who just rushed from a warehouse-sized collection of flights holding caged birds, thrown away by humanity into Ronnie's sphere of responsibility. Not his alone, for there was Ayoka and ever-loyal Jessie. The best of the best was there, he thought, including his candy-pink feathered ass. Imagining that brought a broader smile to his face as he turned on his presidential charm for those gathered.

"Good evening, everyone," Ronnie said. "Would anyone like to offer up words of inspiration?" Several hands went up, including Kasuku's and Ayoka's. They each told an anecdote from their ancestors, their mix of African and indigenous words of wisdom washing away Ronnie's stress, and he saw others relax.

"Thank you. Let's hear celebratory accomplishments from each of our partners and teams."

Ayoka went first, the lead of several of the Pochelani de-extinction teams.

"We had our best year yet for fledglings and have decided to stop the artificial production of new Carolina parakeet lines derived from sun parakeets. We have enough genetic diversity and vigor, along with natural mating and nesting, to grow the flock here until our release sites are ready in a few years. Our avian transgenic process has been a resounding success."

A cheer went up.

"And we have three more indigenous Nations in the alliance committed to planting food and nest flora, and five more national, state, and county parks. It looks like our parakeets, once they're released, won't have any trouble foraging and nesting."

The smiles continued as more departments shared good news, including finance reports of record donations. Ronnie knew the answer, but he asked anyway. "Where is this boost in income coming from?"

The treasurer and board lawyer, Jimmy, said, "It's coming from several areas. Our shared campaign with other movements and organizations, 'None Are Free Until All Are Free,' is helping people understand the interconnections of oppressions between peoples and other species. But the biggest shift has been Life Bequests. This quarter alone we received two donations of over a million dollars each."

The holoed public relations team lead, Jen, joined in. "We've been doing a good job letting people know how their donations help not only their bird, but through our reparations department, indigenous and historically oppressed and marginalized communities, ecosystems, and species. And something else is going on. We've joined up with Multispecies Epidemiological Services and found some possibly startling correlations, which are now being investigated more rigorously before public disclosure."

Ronnie couldn't help but grimace because he knew what was coming, what he'd suspected for years.

Jen continued, "So the good news is we are being given more birds that come with donated money after their owners die, and that means fewer parrots are in homes. The bad news is that we, as always, can't keep up with all the donated birds, because people don't want to keep parrots as much anymore."

"Why is that bad news? Isn't that what we have been going for?" asked one of the newest partners.

"Yes, it is, and we want them to do it because we want their parrots to fly free and have freedom for their lifetimes. But some people with parrots think parrots make them sick, possibly deathly sick. It could be a symptom of the Corona-Flu Syndrome, COFS, with people either impacted by a disease or by chronic stress and oppression that leads to susceptibility to disease, or they think that hurting animals, wildlife, and biodiversity leads to individual perceived manifestations of zoonotic diseases."

"Is that what's happening in New Zealand?" asked Jimmy.

"What is happening in New Zealand? I've been in the flights all day, purposely avoiding tech," explained Ronnie.

"Social media is calling it Zealand Zombie Disease, and there might be something to it because they're in lockdown" said Jen. "I'm keeping an eye on it and will let you know if it's going to impact us."

"Why should it?"

"The AI Conspiracy Index lists birds, and even parrots, as one of the nodes."

"That's all we need, rumors blaming parrots for humanity's failures."

Jessie, the sanctuary lead, looked at Ronnie with an apologetic head tilt. "So, we're already into the challenge part of the meeting?"

Ronnie nodded.

Jessie continued, "Maybe for the same reasons, we can't keep staff and volunteers. We continue to be shorthanded. People don't want to work with caged birds. Plus, we've lost several key employees over the last years, as we all know, heart achingly."

Even the holoed eyes turned to the plaque on the wall with the inscribed names of members, staff, and volunteers who had died over the years, including the latest name, Eddie Martin. Eddie was the love and light of Ronnie's life. The only person he loved more than birds.

"Do you have a solution?" Ayoka asked.

Jessie said, "We can hire more people and raise salaries, and add benefits that Universal Health Care doesn't offer. Our mission is training volunteers, especially from vulnerable populations, to take care of the birds. It also helps them heal from their traumas by being with birds traumatized by captivity. But it might be a model we have to shift from."

Kasuku cleared her throat and sounded nervous. "There may be another way – the USSA. They contacted me recently." Kasuku paused, giving the triggering mention of the USSA time to fade.

"I know their vision is uncomfortable, as succession always is, even if it comes from the left, but the United Solidarity States of America is convincing. They know we're struggling to care for so many birds, and to honor their promise of Unconditional Solidarity, they offered volunteers to help when we need them."

Ronnie thought maybe the USSA was crazy enough to do what had been too hard for so many others. That was their pattern, as Ronnie knew from Eddie's deep involvement with USSA.

"I can run some trial publicity on this with polls and do a financial analysis and get back to you before the next meeting. Will that work?" asked Jen.

"Anyone opposed to at least checking this out?" said Kasuku.

After no one spoke, Ronnie said, "Okay any more challenges or decisions we need to make?"

The meeting continued with challenges and decisions for another hour before Ronnie said, "Time for closing words of inspiration. If I may. Hope may be the thing with feathers, and it asks far more than a crumb from me, from you, and the world. We are here to feed the birds by letting them feed themselves because in doing so we feed our souls, knowing that one day they shall fly free, as shall we all."

"As shall we all," the room replied.

The meeting ended, and Ronnie nodded as he slipped outside into the cold evening. He walked along the path to his small house, built decades ago as the sanctuary had morphed into an intentional community. Once he thought his living space was too small, and now it loomed large with Eddie gone. Behind his house, his family's old farmhouse had been converted to offices and meeting rooms.

He stopped under the oak tree that his great-grandfather had played under as a child, as had he. The oak might have even been home to Carolina parakeets, when the tree was young.

Looking up at the winter stars shining over the Kentucky countryside, he spoke to Orion. "You were thrown into the sea and killed because you boasted that you could rid Earth of all her animals. What is our fate then, we humans, who have mastered destruction? Will we end up like you? Antiheroes and heroes alike, slowly fading into the west. As shall we all? As shall we all."

Chapter 15
Kentucky, USA

"Hruuck, Hruck!" Hercules deeply called as he flew the length of the flight to the large skylight. He said to the stars, "It's good to see you, white feather down drops of my ancestors, sprinkled in all directions. And you, too," he said to the moonlit wispy clouds, "like floating, dancing white feathers in the dark forever." He shook his body, his own faint white cloud arising as two small, down feathers fell to the floor. *I am as those above me, and before me*, he thought. *I shall endure.*

"Wheetee, wheetee!" over and over called the all-white umbrella cockatoo Crazy White One, which started up Crazy White Two and Three, all hanging upside down and rocking. Yellow-head, a sulphur-crested cockatoo, flew to the left, which is most cockatoos' dominant foot, crossing to the side of the cage wire that felt like a hard vine to the birds. She turned in the weak-foot direction, her wingtips brushing the branches where the Pinky Clan was bunched so close together that they looked like one bird with many eyes tracking Orange-head, a citron-crested cockatoo, that began chasing Yellow-head back and forth.

Hercules hung his head almost imperceptibly lower, thinking how this was going to be one of those nights. Out of the corner of his eye, he stared at the flight's surveillance camera, the hard head with a single eye. Tonight, the redeye was closed. His head raised at that. It was stressful to be watched by predators all day, to the point of feeling crazy.

He didn't fly to the highest branch in the cage because that might stimulate his flight companions, whom he referred to as his non-chosen wingteam. Instead, he flew to the hollow tree trunk that curved up. He was angry that wingteammates were one more thing he couldn't control. But, he reminded himself, they were his regardless, and he was theirs.

Hercules stretched himself and lifted his weak foot, catching several of the Pinky Clan eyes, those cockatoos with splashes of pink decorating their solid grey and white feathers. He quickly lowered his foot with a light thwak that could be heard only by some nearby. Raising his strong foot that grasped the drumming stick strung on a hard vine, with resounding force he struck the drumming tree. Its echoes startled everyone in the flight. He struck the drumming tree again, and then once more.

"Drum with me, wingteam! Chenereech!"

A foot emerged from the Pinky Clan ball of feathers, timidly hitting the perch, and then another. Yellow-head cocked her head and fell with a flutter to the closest branch, as if mesmerized by the beat of the many-footed Pinky Clan. Orange-head flew to the opposite side, mistiming her landing and fell to the floor. Stretching erect as if she had choreographed the fall, she lifted her foot and slapped the floor.

"Wheetee, wheetee, what fools we are!" cried Crazy White One, twirling on a rope. The Crazy Whites were always the last to join in and the first to leave a wingteam gathering, but they eventually settled as more and more birds stilled, except for their drumming feet. Yellow-head and Orange-head began to whistle on the offbeat, joined by faint whistles from the small grey crests further down the aisle of flights, the cockatiels often ostracized by the larger cockatoos.

When the wingteam was in rhythm, on the next beat Hercules kept his feet perched as did all the others on that beat, and some on the next. Being locked up meant they got to practice a lot, if nothing else. "Tonight is special. Shorthat has returned." He sought Shorthat's eyes in the corner, but only briefly because he didn't want to trigger Shorthat's seizures. To the corella cockatoo Hercules asked, "Would you tell us about your journey?"

"Wheeeeee, Wheeee!" cried Crazy White Two. "Can't we talk about what we did to the controller today?" he said, referring to Adonis. "We made him scream!"

Seeing that he was going to lose control again, Hercules drummed three times and then held his strong foot in the air as did many of the others, making Crazy White Two angrily gape with an open beak at the assembly that followed Hercules' lead.

"Shorthat?" Hercules prompted.

Shorthat crisscrossed along the nobranch until he was more visible, bowed his head, and lowered his diminutive crest. The others in turn bowed and crested until Shorthat spoke.

"The last time you saw me I was dancing without rhythm on the hard earth, or so some of you told me when I returned today during newlight. All I saw was darkness until I woke, held in the wingtrap by White Controller 2. Ah, I thought, I was in the DeathNoHelp place, where so many of us go and never return, and others come back a little bit better but still not free. I am the latter though. Hsshhpp," he digressed, "I wish I was the former.

I feel like I am caught eternally in an eagle's claw. This is bad enough, but with my black-out illness I am tired and sad. I have spent nearly my entire life here in this hardvinenoforest, never knowing when the darkness will come, and wishing at the same time that it would never leave." He then bowed his head, but didn't crest, a sign of defeat and despair. Two of the Pinky Clan untangled themselves from the others and walked with Shorthat back to the corner.

"Gottagetout, gottagetout, gottagetout!" sounded off the Crazy Whites who flew without intention into one corner and then the next, beaking the hardvines, futilely they knew, but unable to stop.

Hercules began to drum, calling "Crazy Whites" on each upbeat as Yellow-head and Orange-head whistled. This turned Crazy White One's and Two's heads back to the center of the flight, listening. Their bodies followed their eyes as they flew off the walls, leaving Crazy White Three hanging frozen, beaked onto the hardvine and afraid to let go.

"Will you tell us about your journey?" Hercules knew it was a risk to ask them to speak, but if he didn't, no one else might have a chance to tell their story tonight.

Crazy White One lunged at Crazy White Two, "You go." Crazy White One lunged back, saying, "No, you go first." This went on for about 200 heart beats, which Hercules knew because he was counting his breaths to still his urge to sweep down and sink his beak into their crests.

"Oh, all right," they both said at once, beginning their duet, particular to their kind, a faint yet disturbed echo of what their ancestors might have done.

"I hatched in a notreenest, no mother to turn me," began

Crazy White One.

"I hatched in a notreenest box, only seeing mother for a week before I went to a plastic box," said Crazy White Two.

"Hard, hard, notree, notree, not real, not real!"

"Controller hands fed me, groomed me."

"Controller hands loved me, so they said."

"Controller gave me to another."

"Then another and another."

"But where was Mother?"

"Never and evermore no Mother."

"They loved me, they said."

"I love you, I tried to say."

"Then too tired to say."

"Then too angry to stay."

"Now we are here."

"Now, here."

"Nowhere we are."

"Nowhere."

Pinky Clan squeaked, "Nowhere," and a timid foot came down.

Crazy White One and Two hissed, "Nowhere, nowhere," skipping to Pinky Clan, drawing Crazy White Three's eyes and adding wings to the clustered clan. A row of pink and white bowed their heads, uncrested, defeated. *They were not alone in their sorrow*, thought Hercules. He would form a wingteam with them yet.

"Twarrk!" A deep voice called from a high perch closest to the skylight. This was Oldwing, from the high perch given to her out of respect to the one closest to the ancestors of the dark forever.

"Not 'nowhere', not 'now, here', but 'Now! Here!'

Not only did heads look up, but silence stretched beyond their flight down the length of the other wingteams in their separated hardvinenoforest spaces. Many thoughts echoed the same. An old one would speak tonight! Someone who had lived in the Freeforest, a storied place full of heroes and adventures.

Hercules watched Oldwing beak her way down the tilted noperch, limping, and barely able to see the many who moved out of the way as the honored one approached the center of the flight. There was only one other old one still with them, but he had gone to the DeathNoHelp place days ago, and the worst, perhaps the best, was feared.

"Oldwing, would you tell us of your journey?"

"It is not just my journey, but that of all of us. I will tell it so we remember who we are. Long before this controller noforest came into being, there was the true forest. There was no stopping of the sky that went on forever. You didn't need to crane your neck to see a short distance but only look straight up and forever was there for you," Oldwing said as she pointed with her half-bent wing to the sky light. Eyes followed, and more than one head was open beaked.

"You could even fly straight up, as far as you wanted, if you dared the wrath of the great crested eagles." At this, more beaks gaped open, ready to ward off danger. "The only things that blocked far-sight or far-flight were the trees that held up the sky, their green both darker and lighter than the wings of the green shorttails that live three wingteams down from us. In these trees were flowers of all colors, much like the longtails that now live in the separate noforest place that we see when they take down our walls and let us stretch our wings in the sun during the long days.

152

"Imagine no hardvine traps, but a forest of colors, below, above, and all around, as far as you could see and fly. And we did fly far to eat of these many colors and to find trees to love and that would love our children as they hatched into the future. But I didn't think of children during my first feather changes. I was wild, and I was young. I would soar above the arms of trees, so high above, and call loud, daring the eagle, pretending I was Firstbird."

Oldwing was such a good storyteller that beaks around the room shut, except for a few in the Pinky Clan, and heads stretched tall in pride.

"My wingteam flew with me and together we let go of our branch and fell, and fell. The last one to flap was the winner, and almost everyone could be a winner because we played it again and again.

"One day when I was on top of the Freeforest I saw something new. Where there had been colors as far as we could see, there was now a wound out of which dirty feather clouds flew sluggishly up to the sky. My wingteammates and I, thinking this was a game, raced to the horizon. We heard sounds we'd never heard before, loud, angry haunting calls, and saw our first controllers. They were riding on the backs of land eagles, chewing up the trees. They didn't swallow them, but cast them aside to clear the way to take down more and more of our loves. So stunned were we that we didn't see a controller take up a branch and point at us. There was a loud clap, like a tree falling in a storm, and two of my wingteammates fell to the forest floor. It wasn't a game. They never rose again.

"We fled from death and told everyone what we'd seen. Some old ones said they had seen controllers with killing sticks, but to attack the Freeforest so savagely was something new. I never went back to that living scar on the land. Instead, it came to us. Every year it crept toward us, and every year we retreated deeper into the Freeforest. At last, there was nowhere safe because the controllers came with their killing sticks, and more wingteammates lost their lives on the forest floor, too young, too young.

"Then came a greater horror, the sticky controller vines. They wove them up into the beloved trees, trapping one of our kind, calling out in misery. A wingteammate must be given aid when they ask. They caught so many, as if the controllers had a thousand snakes' tongues. During these futile rescue attempts, our wingteam dwindled by the hundreds. Wings were cut short and bodies were thrown as if dead to the controllers below and taken away, never to be seen again.

I was too wise to be caught, thinking of myself as the immortal Firstbird. But then they came for my children. They climbed the tree while I was gathering food, which took nearly an entire day. My children were nearly ready for their firstflight, which they would never attempt. The controllers wrapped a sticky vine around their legs, catching them in branches around our home. When my promisedwingmate and I returned, our children were crying. We had to try to rescue them. I was trapped, as was my promised, and like so many before me, my wings were cut and I disappeared into darkness. I keep looking, but I never saw him or the children again.

"Then began days and days of waking into newlight, but the bad dream never ended. They took me far from my home, and hundreds with me, stuffed into hardvine and notree traps, even into all-see water bottles, which controllers used to trap water's flow. Strangers died all around me before they could become friends, and those that lasted longer, my forcedwingteam dwindled until only a few of us were left. I was taken to my last place before coming here. It was like this building but with much smaller noforest spaces, and with only one wingteammate. He was not my choice, but we learned to love each other, and then our first children came, but the controllers took them. I screamed as I had in the forest, for the loss was grievous.

"I swore I would never have children again. I would not love only to give my children over to a life far from the Freeforest. This made my forcedpromisedwingteammate angry. He chased me back and forth. Such was his wrath, not at me but at our nochoice lives, that one day he caught me and buried his beak into my crest. I disappeared into darkness and woke in a DeathNoHelp place, like the one here. I thought I would die, and I wanted to, though the controllers in all-white poked and prodded me to live. But I had no children, no loving teammates, and no trees. Then one night, a flock of Firstbirds came to me. In the dark, they shone, all the colors of the Freeforest flowed from their wings."

"She had a vision of Firstbirds!" whispered many voices throughout the wingteams. Though the culture of each wingteam was different, every kind had stories of Firstbirds.

"They took me in their wings and nibbled with their rainbow beaks around my wounds. This eased my pain. They said nothing, but when I awoke the next day, I decided to live. The Firstbirds saved my life, though the controllers thought they had. So sure of themselves and their knowledge that after several moon cycles passed, they placed me in a different noforest space with another, who chased me as well. They paired me with another, and then another. I carry as many scars as the Freeforest," she said lifting up her crooked foot and nonbending wing, fused at the old beak break. She didn't need to point to the cruel absence of part of her upper beak, for even their third eyelids couldn't shut out such horror.

"Then one day I was brought here by Controller 1, Hercules's friend, where I have become not a Firstbird, as in my childhood dreams, but a Lastbird, as in my adult waking nightmares." She did not bend her uncrested head at this, but stretched higher, and spoke louder.

"Listen, all of you who fear that the end times have come to you and this wingteam. We may think that we will not outlast this pain, but we can all be Firstbirds. That was what was passed onto me in that dark time. Loss has always come to our kind and kin, and to all life, and yet we endure. Perhaps not us, but through the future children of the Freeforest that is everywhere. Even here in this noforest place with notrees and hard rock noforestground, we are free. And you are heroes," she said, turning slowly, meeting eyes and holding them.

"The Freeforest cannot live without you, for you and yours past and yet-to-come are the seed carriers. In your beaks you carry the young of the forest so that many different trees may grow far and wide. Even your castoffs carry seeds for a better world. Look, now," she said pointing to the hard rock noforestground, plastered with their droppings, "and look within. Even the shit of our life is a gift to the generations. Now! Here! This moment, and not one wing beat later, is our time to rise up and soar. Heroes live not just in stories, but in our hearts. Be the birds you were born to be, be the beauty you are and will always be. Let the telling of our story and the healing of our wounds be the seeds of hope that will grow into the Freeforest of the future. You aren't nowhere, you are here. Now! Here!"

It seemed to Hercules that Oldwing's feathers glowed and she'd grown twice her size. He thought maybe it was just her telling, or maybe she was right. She was not only the Lastbird. She was also the Firstbird, as were they all.

Oldwing teetered over to Hercules, who offered her the drumstick. She placed her arthritic foot over his, "Together we drum."

And so they did, and so did their wingteam, and so did the wingteam next to them and across from them. Long tails, short tails, no tails, cresteds, and not cresteds alike beat a rhythm with feet, calls, and whistles, their noise carrying to the big long tails in the separate noforest beyond theirs. "Guara!" the long tails called, making a sound like their last old one who had known the Freeforest. They marveled, awakening, at least for this one darktime, to their power and their beauty. They drummed, then danced, their calls once heard for miles throughout a thick Freeforest, now carried from one noforest space to another, much like they had in the endtimes when their voices jumped through the fragmented forest patches of their homeland. Noforest after noforest heard the news, stirring their own ancients who flowed in their blood, until at last the farthest noforest heard something new to them. They were the color of sun and flower, this generation engineered by controller hands, but also of those long ago fallen, refined by millions of years of Earth love. They heard for the first time the promise of their past beating in their hearts, an eternal beauty. They were becoming, and this uncaged joy overcame their sense of bewilderment and unanswered grief as they responded as one, "Sakreet!"

LORAKIM JOYNER

Chapter 16
South Australia

Nikau was on his third cup of coffee when three humans, bio-PPEd to the max, were guided into the lab by Daku. He wasn't sure what he was seeing, still snagged by the little snooze he had been enjoying until he heard Jule, exclaim, "Hey, Baraka, did you clone yourself on the way over?"

"Hi, Jule. I probably should have let you know.   They wouldn't let me message you because they were afraid you'd turn them away."

Aria walked closer and sputtered, "Helga, I'll be dammed. I mean Dr. Constantin. What are you doing here?"

"I thought I could be more use here since I can work with AI programs from anywhere.   And Australia's going to have restricted travel, if not from the prion scare, then from the typhoon. If I can't get home, I want to be of the most use I can."

"What typhoon?" Aria said.

"It's still several days away, but they're predicting it might hit here and New Zealand," said Helga.

"Typhoons are hard to predict around Australia, so it's always a long shot to plan anything," said Jule.

"Okay, the typhoon was just an added excuse. I really wanted to be here. But let me show you. Bob, display MASCD results for Australia and New Zealand."

Jule winked at Aria over Helga's ever-present teaching and controlling style. Jule then looked up, "Wow, you're right. The MASCD nonconfirmed social overlay is trending towards red in Australia."

"Bob, show the International Typhoon Tracker in a smaller window," Helga continued.

"Look at that," said Aria about the red arrow on the screen. "The path of typhoon Diwa is predicted to hit southern Australia and then head toward New Zealand's South Island."

"The latest AI from the MASCD results and contact surveys are asking for more input about parrots," Helga began, but not sure she had everyone's attention, paused for them to take in the information. "I thought we could use some help in avian pathology. Do you know Dr. Pereira from Brazil?" She pointed to the third figure in white.

Jule and Aria nodded, and Dr. Pereira said, "Glad to meet you. I've heard so much about your work, Doctors Vogel and Ropata, and Dr. Rewi, too. Please call me Tiago."

Nikau lifted his eyebrow and tilted his head, curious beyond the red, yellows, and oranges on the wall screens and the data from their testing. He couldn't quite place how he knew Tiago.

Tiago said, "I work with Baraka on the biologic and anatomical basis of intelligence, particularly in birds, and especially in parrots. And it goes without saying, in therapod dinosaurs."

Nikau said, "Right. I've read some of your papers. Sorry I missed your talk yesterday. We were a bit busy here."

"That's why I am here. How can I help?"

"First by calling me Nikau." "And me Aria." "And me Jule."

"And me Helga," they each said with a slight bow and quick smile.

Aria directed everyone into the monotony of preparing the new ELISA plates that had the kea prion, PrK. They would be used to test a multitude of samples – more keas, more parrots, more birds, more humans. Some samples they had and many were due to arrive throughout the day and the next.

"While you're doing that, I'm going to recalibrate the PMCA reader to give the world an automatic test for detecting PrK," said Aria. "And heaven forbid we ever need it."

"I'm pretty good with medical diagnostic equipment," volunteered Daku, "since some of our readers are older."

They worked like a hive, and later that morning their first test results were completed. As the last result posted on the screen, Luther haloed in to join the other halos who'd been coming and going all morning.

"Looking at all the positive results, I think I know what this means. But how is everyone else interpreting this?" asked Luther.

"Bob, please unmask the codes to show the sample source," said Aria. They had hidden where the samples came from in order to remove human bias and test for controls.

As codes faded into sample sources, it became clear that PrK was found in every kea tested, and most of the parrots in New Zealand and Australia, but not in any other kinds of birds.

"Seems clear, at least if these preliminary tests hold true, we have a parrot prion, PrK, and it crosses species in its occurrence. Did you know that a kea prion occurred in other parrots?" Luther turned towards Aria.

"No, though we should have. I should have," she said, lowering her eyes.

"Maybe it's new. Maybe we didn't see it before because it wasn't in other parrot species before. Or in humans, for that matter," Helga said.

"When will the first human samples be finished?" asked Luther.

"About 5 p.m., and then it'll be staggered after that," said Aria, looking at her notes.

"Okay, let's not make any new official recommendations until we get those results, right?" Luther looked up and tapped his question into the chat for the many nonpresent team members. Virtual and nonvirtual heads bobbed in agreement, and no one in the chat disagreed.

Later in the afternoon, Jule saw Aria elbow-deep in PMCA reader components and asked, "How is it going?"

"I still can't get the reader to replicate in the volumes we need, so I'm making sure the reader's electronics aren't fritzing out," she said as she waved the disassembled incubation chamber. It fell and clanged loudly on the floor. "That's not going to help," she said inspecting it. "Looks okay." She set it down and rubbed her eyes. "Maybe I should take a nap." She looked longingly at the living quarters.

"Before you go, I wanted to let you know that we got most of the results from the human samples that Luther sent over, including Callum's. I had the source codes revealed for the finished ones. I wanted you to know before the data goes up on the screen."

"He's got it, doesn't he?"

"He does."

"You know, I'm almost relieved. At least we have an explanation for his unexpected decline. But I don't know how he and Isaac contracted it. It's not like they've been eating keas. It must be transmitted differently than BSE, but how? You'd think if they had it, as much as Mom and I work with keas, we'd have it too."

"You mother tested positive."

"But she's not showing any symptoms." They both stared at each other. "Okay. But I am," she squeaked out, her chest tight. She wanted to appear calm as her hands trembled and she bowed her head as if inspecting the dismantled incubation chamber on the lab bench.

"Aria, we still don't know what this means. Many people in New Zealand tested positive. Half of them showing various symptoms didn't have PrK in their blood, so that means that they have something else, or perhaps nothing at all. You know how COFS works. We are seeing symptoms of emerging diseases everywhere, even when there's no way a person could have been exposed. We also have some humans without symptoms but testing positive for PrK, as do others with symptoms in the same household."

"You're right. But we have to test ourselves, and, heck, a lot of people. We need a lot more PMCA readers," she said, still looking down at the scattered parts.

As if on cue, Luther audioed in. "Sorry I couldn't be there in person. I'm on my way back from a satellite clinic we set up for initial testing. I'm in a low band-width zone in the mountains, but I can see the results. Could you reveal the sample sources, without the humans' names?"

Team members made various points, repeating much of what Aria and Jule had just discussed. They then queried the Prion AI that they'd named Carol. Carol recited monotonically,

"There is an 85% chance that PrK is causing a transmissible spongiform encephalopathy in humans. Mode of transmission unknown."

"Does it cause disease in any other species?" asked Helga.

Aria was wide awake waiting for Carol's response.

"Insufficient data. Testing in only three kea brain samples, all negative for tissue damage."

"What does the Zoonotic Global Surveillance Consortium and the International Emerging Zoonotic Disease Working Group suggest we do, as well as our colleagues at the World Health Organization and the CDC?" asked Luther.

"Can we go to break-out rooms and reconvene in an hour?" a disembodied voice asked, but the screen flashed the name of Dr. Anand.

"Done," Helga and Luther said at the same time, more intrigued with each other than irritated. Like a fruit-basket-upset, holos disappeared and others appeared.

Aria, nap long forgotten, pinged Luther, "Callum and Mom tested positive. Have you told them?"

He responded, "No. Waiting to see what this working group makes of it first, and also to get your opinion. Sorry this is so close to home for you."

Aria's throat clenched her sob. "I want to be on the call when you tell them. What about possible treatments?"

"We know it's all palliative. There's no cure for prion diseases, though we are getting closer. We're treating Isaac with various combinations of dementia alleviating drugs. And now that we have identified the agent as PrK, we can work on a molecular solution to block the prions from misfolding or attaching or clumping in the nervous system. It's all experimental at this stage I'm afraid, as is any possible vaccine."

"But Mom has no symptoms?"

"We didn't do a thorough examination. Tomorrow we'll run a full battery of neurological tests for any evidence of disease on her and others who tested positive."

"Tomorrow? How about today? Not just for me and my family, but for everyone. Let's call them after we hear from the break-out rooms. Will that work for you?"

"Of course."

Aria and Luther joined their break-out rooms, Aria to the avian disease group, and Luther to the human dimension one. People moved in and out between rooms to cross-fertilize the discussion and inform others of conclusions. Aria pinged Nikau to meet by the living quarters, where they could relax some of the laboratory protective clothing regulations, and enjoy food and water intake.

"How are you holding up?" she asked.

"Short on sleep, like everyone else. You?"

"Two of those positive human samples were Kora and Mom."

"Oh no, Aria. You must be worried sick."

"I want to tell you, I have a problem with balance. I thought it was just a hangover from New Year's, but I'm clumsier than usual."

"But you don't have any other signs?" Nikau looked closely at her.

"No. But you should know since we don't know how it's transmitted. That's three in my family, and now me."

"I think I'm safe since your family is a secret cult that eats kea body parts in ritual to honor the great kea god to which I've not been initiated. I should be okay. Also, you didn't bite me very hard the other night," he said, taking her hand.

She pulled her bare hand away. "Seriously, we should minimize contact until we figure this out. So far, no keas have shown symptoms or pathological lesions. They don't seem to get sick from it. Some other risk factors are at play, some unknown transmission modality."

"Are you dumping me?"

"No, I'm loving you."

"It's not like we've had much opportunity for a romantic evening on a pristine Australian beach anyway. Usually the hero exits after getting bit by a zombie and either getting zombified or dying protecting their beloveds. I don't think we're there yet in this conference-turned-thriller. We'll see it through together."

They pulled on their gloves and embraced, the bio-PPE protecting their bodies, but not their hearts. They reluctantly released each other when messaging directed everyone to report to the main room.

"Human disease group. What have you got?" asked Luther.

"We don't know anything really, but we'll know a lot more after extensive testing for both PrK and the disease in the general population and those who have been around parrots. Anyone who tests positive will go through a series of diagnostic tests for symptoms," reported Dr. Anand.

"This isn't going to give us definitive answers because the symptoms are generalized, and it's hard to get a confirmed diagnosis without biopsying brain tissue," said Luther.

"Yep, it's a bitch of a disease. Let's keep doing what we started with the New Zealand samples but expand the testing. With greater numbers we'll have greater confidence about what's going on and what we need to do," said Helga.

Aria raised an eyebrow at Helga's choice of expressions, both in sharp words and sharp glances at Luther. Was Helga being her domineering and challenging self, always with a hint of affection and respect for others? But she seemed more intent on Luther than anyone else.

Aria said, "I can send the PrK back to New Zealand and anywhere else. We can share my calibration settings on the PMCA reader so we can test rapidly and quickly."

"Carol, what is the morbidity rate of those who work with parrots in Australia and New Zealand and haven't been tested?" asked Luther.

Carol recited, "Insufficient information. There is no retrospective analysis at this point. Based on recent MASCD surveys and current results...calculating..."

Helga said, "While we're waiting, let's hear from the avian disease group."

Aria said, "We need to know how the PrK gets into humans. We have to assume that not all the people have been eating keas," and smiled at Nikau.

"What's your best hypothesis of where it came from and how it infected humans?" Luther asked.

Aria said, "We'll be studying this for years probably, but it seems, with the cross-reactivity between the PrScrapie and PrK, that keas were infected by eating contaminated sheep carcasses and the prion mutated in them."

"Why isn't it causing symptoms in keas and other parrots?" Helga asked.

"I'm just guessing here," said Aria, "but birds have a natural salt bridge in their prion proteins that protects them from replicating into misfolded proteins that cause the disease. Basically, they are immune to prion diseases."

"Makes sense," said Dr. Armand. "Stabilizing proteins through the salt bridge is a mode of experimental treatment, as well as prevention in mammals and could be part of the solution here and for vaccines."

"So, prion replicates in birds, but doesn't hurt them?" pressed Luther.

"Yes, various prions exist naturally in birds and other species, and can even have beneficial impacts," said Aria.

Luther said, "So how does it transmit to humans?"

Jule said, "Environmental factors are always a possibility. Human illness seems to occur in contact with keas or other parrots, so maybe it's in the body fluids, excretions, or feather dander that humans come in contact with, either directly with the bird or through a contaminated environment. It infects humans through some mechanism, like accidental ingestion, rubbing your eyes, or an open wound. I can run the environmental samples I collected. Then we can set up the calibrated PCMA readers to test humans, parrots, and environmental samples anywhere we like."

"Public advisory and surveillance group, what have you got?" said Helga.

Their rep, Roger Case, in his best suit, said as if speaking to a jury, "We are still so early in our understanding, but Australia is nearly red with the social overlay. Although we don't yet have any confirmed cases in Australia, we should officially shut down Australia. Our group wants to schedule a press conference as soon as possible."

Aria thought Roger looked like a lawyer on every soap opera

ever produced.

Carol recited, "End calculating. The background morbidity and mortality rate of people who have some connection to parrots is higher than those who have not, after controlling for other factors."

Jule and Nikau moved towards Aria, seeking comfort for themselves as much as offering it to her. Helga, Tiago, and Baraka didn't look comfortable. In fact, no one did.

Helga said, "I hate to say this, but the infection may reach beyond just Australia and New Zealand. People have been legally and illegally moving keas out of New Zealand for over a century. They're all over the world, in parks and zoos, and private collections."

"So clearly we need to broaden our testing and surveillance to other countries," said Luther.

Aria said, "Do you know how many people have parrots, or have had parrots in the world? Hundreds of millions. Every continent but Antarctica has at least one kind of parrot, in nature or in cages."

Roger said, "We were suggesting informing the public only about Australia and New Zealand. Announcing broad testing could cause a global shutdown and panic, economically and otherwise."

Helga said, "Let's do preliminary and private testing now. We've got parrot experts in this room from several continents, and others are in downtown Adelaide. It's not a big sample size, but it's a start."

"And as we announced about New Zealand, we can say there may be a link between parrot contact and – hell – what are we calling the disease?" said Roger.

"We'll have to be vague since we don't have much to go on at this point. How about Parrot Prion Disease Syndrome, PPDS," suggested Luther.

"We can say that currently it's been found only in New Zealand. However, authorities are shutting down Australia as a precaution because they're in the same communicable disease travel bubble," said Roger.

Daku said, "There are going to be a lot of unhappy commerce and government types."

"Thank goodness we don't have to rely on them to make decisions for the greater good," said Nikau. "Other countries learned that during the COF years. There was little to no trust in governments to do the right thing, despite high mortality rates. After COF, a rush of new laws established an independent governmental organization that issued alerts and recommendations." Nikau looked to Aria, asking with his eyes if he was preaching to the choir. She smiled.

Helga said, "You both raise a point about the governments as a necessary part of our work and decisions. We have liaisons to both countries. Do you agree with our next steps?"

"Yes, we've patched in the Australian prime minister's office and they've scheduled a press conference in an hour," said Roger.

Luther said, "Okay, good work, team. Let's keep the holo and audio lines open, and, Adelaide IDL folks, it looks like you could use some rest."

"Thanks, Luther. We'll decide how to delegate our work here and in other locations and let you know."

"Kia ora, one and all!"

"Kia ora."

No sooner had the holos winked out than the in-person

teams rushed together. Daku said, "I messaged a tech to come draw everyone's blood."

"So, it's now a vampire as well as zombie film plot," said Nikau.

"And a weather disaster film," said Tiago studying the weather display.

Diwa's center was darker red, a Category 4. The storm and the future churned faster toward them than anyone had thought possible a few short days ago.

LORAKIM JOYNER

Chapter 17
La Moskitia, Honduras

Kaskatara, like Australia and New Zealand, was also on lockdown, but for different reasons. The gun fight that stopped most normal activity began on a day when Orlin and Jaora awoke under a towering ceiba, an ancient tree who had provided a nesting cavity for the last great green macaws. It was a shrine, and a rendezvous and hiding place. Both men had been laying low from Lucero's assassins at this far outpost of the village. Beyond the outpost was territory they could no longer protect, and the deforestation each year came closer to home. But there was still a sizable patch of forest nearby on the western slopes of what, in their youth, was called the Colon Mountains. Not wishing to honor a symbol of genocidal colonialism – Christopher Columbus, known as Colon in Spanish – the indigenous territory had unofficially renamed it to *los Apus*, Miskitu for macaws. Others with a stronger Spanish influence called the mountains the Guaras, also indigenous for macaws. It was an important place for their people, "But enough," Orlin told Jaora. "Let's go. I'm worried about Kaskatara and the people."

"And I'm tired of your camp cooking," said Jaora, already packed.

They left the sacred spot and memorial of stones and began

the long walk home. They made good time in the dry season, using the quickest and surest paths. They had to watch out for the smoldering wildfires that each year began earlier and lasted longer due to the increasingly dry climate. On the outskirts of the village, by the river, they heard voices rushing toward them on the tapir path and hid. It was one of the parrot ranger teams.

"Pssst! *Naksa muchachos*," Orlin whispered. "What's happening?"

The youngest Saliwas boy, Jimy, jumped a foot in the air. The men and women in the patrol grinned, and after a few seconds Jimy smiled also, glad to see Orlin and Jaora.

"We spotted Lucero's band of twelve coming this way. They're not far behind us. They mean to harm the village because they couldn't find you and Jaora," said Jimy.

"I think it's time to tell them where we are. Right?" said Jaora.

"Yes, let's end this child's game. I've been doing this my whole life. When they come in the day as if they owned the territory, threatening our families without fear of consequences, it's time to make them afraid," said Orlin, motivating himself as well as others for inevitable violence.

"It'll be six against twelve, so we can't spare anyone to warn the village," said Jimy's father, Geraldo.

"There isn't time. Let's go!" commanded Orlin.

The patrol turned and moved as one back down the path in silence, listening for signs that the gang was approaching them. They heard the soft cluck of a scarlet macaw above them, and they stepped off the path and into the bush as quietly as the ghosts of their ancestors who had hunted the land for generations.

Unfortunately, Lucero's men had also heard the macaw and shot at the bird and the trees. The patrol returned fire, neither group getting a good view of the other, but that didn't stop them from terrorizing each other with shots and insults echoing through the trees.

A vicious voice down the path shouted, "We're hungry, so we're leaving for now. But after breakfast we'll return with more people, and your village will pay. For dinner, those of you still alive will cook your stores for us. And your guaras will be delicious!"

Orlin heard them stalk away, but suspicious of a ruse he pointed at Jimy to retrieve the fallen guara. Jimy soon returned with his patrol shirt wrapped around the wide-eyed macaw, its feathers fluffed as if a chick. One wing was bloodied. Orlin, having already conferred with Geraldo, told Jimy, "Run fast. Take the guara to Kendi. Warn them. We'll post guards around the village. Tell them to send us more help."

"And breakfast," joked Jaora.

Jimy took off running as Orlin said to Jaora, "I don't think Lucero's men had breakfast with them either. They were bluffing. They're probably as miserable as we are playing this game of tapir-no-tapir."

No meals appeared and much time passed, but finally replacements arrived. Orlin and Jaora felt it was safe to go see their families. Kendi saw them from her high porch, where a host of macaws perched, watching over the injured macaw and the village. "Papa's here," Kendi shouted to Ketura and Lapta who were watching a film using solar-powered batteries in the backroom. Not waiting for them, she rushed down the stairs, not even pausing to put on her *chalecas* as she ran to Orlin and Jaora.

Normally reserved in public, Orlin and Kendi embraced. Soon Ketura and Lapta joined them, and then village families, with parrots swirling above them.

As they walked up the stairs to their home, outside of earshot of the children, Orlin said to Kendi, "We challenged them this time. I don't think we can go back to the way it was."

"It's always been desperate with everything at risk. That is why I tell our people we must risk everything. I sent word for help to the council about our situation. Some will come, and then we must make a decision about independence," said Kendi.

"Oh, my little political creature, ever plotting and planning. I am proud of you, and relieved to see you."

"Oh, my forest fighter, always hunting and being hunted. I am proud of you, and so very glad to see you again."

"How is the injured macaw?"

"We set the wing, but I don't know if she'll ever fly again. She's out of danger, as much as any of us are."

"Who is she?"

"She's from one of Rak's earlier clutches. Rak and her current fledglings haven't left the porch since Jimy brought her in."

"I see the liberation cage still has this year's chicks."

"We were set to release them this morning, until we heard shots in the forest. It's not a good time to have naïve flyers around the village."

"But if we get overrun, they'll be trapped here."

"I left the cage doors unlocked, and someone from the liberation team is always nearby to open the doors if needed, and to carry the nonflyers into the forest. We won't lose one more macaw or one more Miskitu today, or any day to come!"

"Save your speeches for later. I'd like a kiss instead." They moved into the shadows of the kitchen, the rush of heat not all from the wood fire and stoves.

The village moved back into more or less a routine, living off the stores in their homes. Only patrollers went to the farms to keep Lucero's growing army from burning their crops and to bring back enough yucca, plantains, and other fresh foods to supplement the rice and beans. On the third day, no one had entered the village, and even the numbers of parrots dwindled. "It's like everyone is afraid to come here," said Yessenia, taking a break in Kendi's porch hammock with a hot coffee. "Even the birds. What have you heard?"

Kendi said, "Not being able to leave the village to get a strong enough signal, we've had to rely on climbing our watch tower. But enough messages came through that we know the council is coming soon to finish what we didn't last week."

"What about help from the military or the government?"

"We won't go back to working with them. They can't be trusted. Five hundred years of colonial rule, and we finally learned our lesson."

Jimy's brother David ran into the village shouting, "They're coming!"

"Who's coming?" said Kendi and Yessenia together, thrusting their coffee cups into the wash basin.

"Everyone!"

Kendi and Yessenia moved according to the plan: first, protecting the children, second, preparing to release the parrots and hide them, and, third, checking their rifles were within reach. A group stepped from the forest into the clearing.

"It's the president of the federation. He came!" said Kendi, mostly relieved but aware of the complicated political moves that always followed him like a stubborn shadow.

"And look, the entire council is with him, and half their villages!" Yessenia said as she stared in awe at the endless crowd that streamed along the path.

Kendi hurried to meet them, "*Naksa, naksa*, everyone. You are so very welcome."

The president, Kenneth, said, "I don't think you will welcome everyone. Lucero's people are right behind us, and they're armed. But so are we," he said, touching the pistol under his shirt. "It's best to have the meeting right away to avoid an incident."

One of the council members, an elder from a village closer to Kirtira, said, "We brought plenty of food. Where can we set up?"

"We can use the church and common area," said Kendi, who with Yessenia began to organize the villagers and newcomers. An hour later, after appetites were satisfied, people were still arriving, and a tense hum rose louder every minute. But there was a hush when Lucero stepped into the clearing, flanked by armed bodyguards. Behind him marched the local military commander and other nebulous military types, some in ski masks.

A shudder went through Kendi, not from fear, but from what she sensed was a critical moment in her people's history. Today they would all fall or rise together. Kendi motioned to David, "Who has the best phone and signal receiver in the village?"

"That would be Jimy."

"Go get him and a few others. Tell them to climb the watch tower and begin filming, live. Whatever happens here today, the world will witness it as well. We won't disappear without our story being told."

Kenneth asked Kendi, "We can start now. But where are the macaws and other parrots?"

"It's strange. We haven't seen much of them."

"So, they choose to stay away? You didn't make them go?"

"Why would we do that? The flyers can take care of themselves."

"You haven't been following the news about parrots then?"

"What news? It's hard to get a signal in the village."

Kenneth handed over his phone that showed a video of a kea flock chewing on cars and sheep carcasses with the words, "*Enfermedad Mortal de Loros Cierra Australia y Nueva Zelanda.*" Something shifted in Kendi but she didn't have time to clarify what the news meant because Kenneth signaled for Kendi to climb with him to the top of her porch so their voices would carry over the crowd. At the top, she saw the village rangers come out of the forest, and some encircled the crowd. They were far outnumbered, but their message was clear. Anyone who started violence would be met with the same.

"Let's start with a prayer, Pastor Lopez?"

During the long prayer, Kendi looked around to honor the love she felt for her people. She wished Orlin was by her side, but he had a job to do, and so did she. She saw the young people on the watch tower were recording, hopefully some of it being broadcast live, and that people were stationed by the liberation cage. Oddly, no visitors thronged there to get a closer look at the caged macaws, nor were any liberated parrots in the trees. She wondered if the gunfire and strangers had scared them off.

After the last amen, Kenneth began, "You know why we have

gathered here. The council will vote on how we'll govern ourselves. Will we join the Communitarian Nation of Miskitu? Or will we merge with the Renewed Federation of Central America, of which Honduras will become a member this year? We have each met with our villages and held countless meetings. Before the vote, let's hear from our vice-president Kendi.

Kendi stepped forward. "You've heard my words before and for those who haven't, hear them now echo in your heart. For too long we've been oppressed by those in power, after taking our power from us. We've been the puppets of those with wealth, after they took what we value from us. We've lost nearly everything. We will not lose any more to the corrupt enemies of peace. You know who they are. They are among us today. Look at your neighbors now. Let your eyes tell them that the day has come when we say, "No more!" Today we are our own people, us, here, expressing with our vote *Solidaridad Incondicional* for all people and all life."

She paused to give them a chance to make eye contact, knowing violence could be subdued and political will encouraged when people saw the humanity in one another – as well as the animality, she thought as she looked up at the skies, longing to see the missing guaras.

The crowd nervously jostled, afraid to make eye contact with others. Even in the same village, there was no consensus. Some were benefitting from the corrupt system, and if things changed, so might their fortunes, or at least that's what they feared. Kendi couldn't tell which way the vote would go, or what the immediate effect of the vote would be.

"It's time for all 27 villages of the territory to vote. Would one council member from each village please come forward?

There will be no secrecy. All will see how we vote," boomed Kenneth.

As the council members made their way forward, faint music and chanting could be heard approaching the clearing. Heads craned to hear the words and see who the newcomers were. "SI! SI! *Solidaridad Incondicional! SI! SI A Toda los Seres, Vida Tierral!*"

They were loud, but Kendi didn't see many of her *compañeros* as the newcomers filled in the edges of the gathering. All shades of humanity were represented, a mix of genetic lines and political leanings. In the clearing, the Lapatistas grew quiet, their model of listening and solidarity exemplified through their actions.

Lucero's glared at those who were in his pocket, including some of the council gathered at the front. His intent was clear to everyone. He would only accept a vote to stay with Honduras where his corrupt officials held sway. Even with witnesses and video cameras rolling, he could spin the story that others had started the fighting. He had instructed his men to target Kendi first and then the counselors who betrayed him. Those deeper in the forest would ambush the rangers along the clearing's edges. The councilors shrank under his stare. They had received death threats that included their families and children. They tore their eyes away from him when Kenneth called for a vote.

"All those in favor of staying with Honduras, raise your hands." A murmur spread over the crowd when many hands raised. "Now all of those who want to leave Honduras and be part of the Miskitu Nation, raise your hands." He paused. "A few of you have not voted. You must vote. This is your duty to the people."

He recounted the vote, an even split.

In this case the tie breaker went to the executive council. Turning to the secretary/treasurer, he asked with his eyes and she responded, "I vote for the Nation."

Kendi let out the breath she didn't know she was holding. She hadn't been sure of the secretary.

"And I vote for Honduras," said Kenneth. Kendi sucked in air, and the crowd gasped. Kenneth turned to Kendi in apology. "I can't risk the lives of so many."

Now it was up to Kendi, and everyone knew how she would vote. The councilors moved back into the crowd, and hands moved closer to weapons. She thought they weren't going to let her vote, and her chronic despair intensified.

"Grrauereck, grrauereck" shattered the silence and ear drums. First one scarlet macaw appeared over the canopy, then ten, and then a hundred, landing in all the trees around the clearing. They kept coming and coming, along with yellow-naped amazons, mealys, and red-loreds. The parrots numbered over a thousand, and still they came, crowding each other on Kendi's roof and the village roofs. Rak flew to Kendi's shoulder and two yellow-napes to her other shoulder. "You came, my beloveds! *Tiki pali.*"

And then the parakeets arrived, swooping and diving low, as if targeting Lucero, who, despite his resolve, ducked and covered his head. He'd heard the news out of New Zealand, and he was afraid. Others were also afraid, while others cried in awe, cheered, and more than a few prayed. The rush of wings and the rustle of feathers blended with parrot calls that smoothed the discordant human drama.

"Such a symphony has never been heard before!" said one journalist into her smart watch.

182

Council members stepped up. "I want to change my vote!" "Me too!" "We vote for the Nation!"

"I too change my vote," said Kenneth. "It's unanimous. Kendi?"

"*Mama* Guara *Tara*! *Mama* Guara *Tara*!" began one voice, then hundreds.

The parrots joined in, their voices and colors adorning the village like flowers and leaves of a forest, united as one biotic community.

Stepping forward, spreading her arms wide as more macaws alighted on them, Kendi spoke slowly and with a flash of defiance in her eyes, "I vote with the people and the parrots. SI!"

Chret and Reta, flew towards Kendi, wing to wing, but realizing there was nowhere to perch on her, they smacked into her. One clung to the top of her head, and the other swung upside down on her braid.

Laughter erupted from the crowd. Their calls of Pree Palisa and their joy flew free to join with others in all corners of Earth through the boys' live streaming video, which both captivated and liberated millions.

LORAKIM JOYNER

Chapter 18
Kentucky, USA

Ronnie awoke for the third morning in a row more tired than before he slept. The news out of New Zealand and Australia had rocked the parrot world, and he woke each day to fewer volunteers and more birds abandoned at the sanctuary's gate. No PPDS cases had been confirmed outside of Australasia, but it didn't take much to set people off. He imagined there might have even been more killings of parrots if not for the video that had gone viral out of La Moskitia. People were, more than ever, on the side of wildlife and the oppressed communities where parrots lived. It was a shift that had been slowly developing over the last decades. The video accelerated and galvanized that trend, and US, USSA, SI!, and the Lapatista movements had seen a sharp increase in membership, donations, and commitment. He had to admit he was even moved himself. He had thought he was too cynical to ever feel Eddie's fervor. And he knew he was too old to care for so many birds and run PACT. He was able to do it only because the USSA had arranged volunteer shifts.

He walked to the Carolina parakeets. They were well isolated from the rest of the captive flock to reduce the diseases that were both confirmed and suspected in many other birds. Over the years there had been several outbreaks of various infectious diseases without warnings, resulting in parrots dropping dead in the other buildings. Ronnie knew that was the product of mixing wildlife from different regions and continents, all thanks to the parrot trade.

He didn't really mind, especially when he wasn't busy, the shower he had to take in the transition room before entering one of the Carolina buildings. There were multiple buildings of parakeets to keep birds separate in case of an outbreak or natural disaster. PACT was also breeding smaller flocks in other parts of the USA, unknown to the public for security reasons. But the biggest and best-known effort was here, one he was proud of, and one he was worried about. For the last few nights, he had dreamed incessantly of the parakeets, and once thought he'd been wakened by their calls.

The hot shower felt good after trudging through mud and the last night's snow. It was cold, the sun hadn't risen. But this January morning wasn't like they'd been when the sanctuary opened years ago. Then blizzards trapped them in with the birds for days at a time. Now he felt almost comfortable in shorts year-round.

Pre-sunrise was his favorite time to visit the parakeets, before any staff appeared and when the birds were most active. "Good morning, Carolina!" he boomed as he walked down the aisle. The birds couldn't hear him or see him. They were enclosed in special nanotechnology web walls, where all that the parakeets saw and felt was a slightly movable mesh that looked like trees and leaves. He wished they could afford this for all their birds, but it was prohibitively expensive and still experimental. The effect of nanotech was that not only did the birds not see themselves in an unnatural cage, neither did he. He felt like he was moving with them through an Eastern forest, like his great-grandparents had done centuries ago.

He listened attentively to their calls, concerned about a difference in tone over the past week. One of his many worries was the birds would learn some human trait that would impact their ability to survive outside, and also, he had to admit, delay or end the release program for this first batch of keets. He made a mental note to check with the de-extinction team later today. They had a whole protocol for language and learning, using AI's to simulate what they thought this species of parakeet would sound and act like from their closest living relative, the sun parakeet. There were no audios of the species in existence, so they had to start from scratch. They had come a long way from the first attempts of recreating Carolina parakeets in the film *The New World*. Constantly developing tech had created not just computer-generated keets but the real thing, almost. They would never get a pure Carolina parakeet, but each generation got closer and closer.

Lost in his mix of old and new world thoughts, he jumped when his phone cried out the same call he was hearing live. "Meatloaf," he said to his phone, "connect to PACT's private meeting room."

Ayoka and Kasuka were in the room, as were Jessie, Jen, and Jimmy. "Good morning, everyone. What's the occasion? It can't be my birthday. You missed that last month."

"Ronnie, have you seen the video?" asked Jen.

"You mean the one of La Moskitia? It's marvelous."

"No, not that one. And it was great," said Jen. "I was working on how to spin it, but that'll have to wait. We have bigger problems."

Ronnie said, "What's up?"

"You need to watch the clip. It's only a few minutes. Somebody leaked it out of the IDL in Adelaide, where the news first broke about the Parrot Prion Disease Syndrome," said Ayoka.

"Okay, what I am looking at?" asked Ronnie as the holovideo appeared in front of him.

"This is the lab, and you'll recognize a few of the people."

"Hey, that's Helga Constantin and Jule Vogel. They consulted with us on setting up the parakeet project and visited just a few years ago. Who else is there?"

"You're looking at Aria Ropata and Nikau Rewi from New Zealand, Tiago Pereira from Brazil, and Baraka Mbungo from the United Kongo Republics."

"Wow, those are all big names in parrot work. What are they doing?"

"They're running samples to test for the prion, PrK, in their own blood. Listen now."

"Our plates are now ready to read," said Aria. "This should be the last batch using our long-hand process. After this we can use the PMCA reader for everything. Does anyone want to keep their results private?"

"No? Okay, I'll go first."

Aria walked over to the lab bench where the six plates had been processed. Ronnie saw her look for the plate that had her code on it, and the holo camera showed what Aria saw, the plate's wells were bright red.

"What does that mean?" asked Ronnie.

"That she's positive. Overwhelmingly so," answered Ayoka.

Ronnie saw her stumble walking to the ELISA reader. Jule and Nikau rushed to her, and all three together inserted the plate.

It confirmed the high concentration in her circulatory system. "I'm so sorry," said Jule as she walked Aria back to the others sitting on lab stools.

"I'll go next," said Nikau. He went to the bench, and the holo camera couldn't pick up any color. The reader showed it as a negative.

Aria smiled at him. Jule took her turn, then walked with a red plate to the reader.

"Another positive," said Ronnie out loud to make sure he understood the video.

"Jule is from Germany?" asked Jen.

"Yes, but she's worked a long time in Australia," said Jessie.

Next went Helga. Positive. Baraka. Positive. Taigo. Positive. Ronnie could see their expressions were the same as his, growing stupefaction with each positive result. He thought it must be a consolation that they had each other. They hugged and the video faded to black.

"They haven't made the results official yet?" asked Ronnie.

Ayoka said, "No, they're still saying the only positive cases are in Australasia, and physically they are there."

"But among them, they cover other continents. This means that the parrot prion could be anywhere, it could be here..." Ronnie's voice faltered.

"Which explains why we were asked to submit results for testing," said Kasuka. "The PrK was delivered to Cincinnati last night. We'll get results in a few hours."

"Jessie, where are you?"

"I'm in the clinic building, reviewing the logs of stored samples."

"I'll meet you there. We need to send over sun and Carolina

samples as well," Ronnie said, moving back to the shower.

"And us? Shall we test ourselves?" asked Jessie.

"It would open up a ton of legal messiness for us if you do, especially without a medical doctor's oversight. No one even knows what the disease is and what a positive test means," said Jimmy.

"Okay. So officially we aren't testing ourselves," said Ronnie for the record, but already planning to sneak in his own sample with the parrots'.

"Oh hey, look, MASCD just tripped off an alert. It says anyone who's worked with parrots should get tested and fill out the surveys," said Jessie.

"Oh my God," said Jen, "social media is blowing up. They're calling it the Zealand Zombie Disease."

"It's only going to get crazier, so let's do this now," said Ronnie as he stepped into the shower.

An hour later the samples were packed. Ronnie grabbed the box. "I'll take them to Cincinnati."

"Are you sure? You can send them on the sanctuary drone," said Jessie.

"I want to see this through and make sure there's no mix-up." And he wanted to make sure they tested his blood as well. He didn't want the hassle of stopping by a human diagnostic lab, knowing how crazy they get during pandemic scares.

"I'd like to go, too." Jessie's face softened with desire, some of it from wanting to help take some of the weight off Ronnie's shoulders, some for Ronnie himself. Ronnie said, "I'll be fine. I'll take the sanctuary smart car. And you're needed here. The new USSA volunteers are still green, and we're still short-handed."

"Okay. I'll see you later today."

"Therapod start," said Ronnie as he stepped up to the car. "Drive to the Cincinnati Wildlife Disease Lab."

"Traffic is heavier than usual and is trending towards even heavier congestion," said Therapod.

Ronnie looked at the map and saw some roads outlined in red, all leading to the major urban hospitals. He had seen this kind of rush with every disease scare that came through. He wished people would learn that in most cases the alerts amounted to nothing. But he couldn't deny that sometimes they did amount to something.

He used his time in the car to address the thousands of messages that were coming in from people urgently wanting to donate parrots and asking questions about the parrot prion. Drafting a standard reply message from his cloud-mail account, he sent it to the sanctuary and PACT accounts he shared with the board and staff. He advised them to not make any decisions until the researchers learned more about the prion.

Something caught his eye as he neared the Ohio river. "Oh my god," he gasped. Two large, long-tailed, red-and-green macaws flew by him in the opposite direction as he crossed the Carter bridge. People were releasing their parrots, in the winter. It was an unusually warm winter, but still his blood pressure was rising at witnessing such cruelty.

He switched to social media, setting his filters to parrots, prion, zombie, and his location. Suddenly his phone was vomiting information on the car's internal screens. "Oh my god, what a shit storm!"

"The weather is clear, and you have arrived at your destination," Therapod informed him.

He looked up and saw a packed parking lot and a line leading into the disease lab. He called the main desk and was routed to the AI who determined that his samples had priority and directed him to another entrance.

"Hey, Ronnie, I thought you'd send your drone after today's traffic forecast. Not to mention the MASCD social overlay recommended no travel," said Bill.

"Everything went to hell in a hand basket quicker than I thought. Here's our samples. How long will take?"

"A couple of hours."

"Have you gotten any positive results?"

"You know I can't tell you that. But hey, I can recommend you to the regional CDIT team. In fact, your group should have already been on it."

"Sure, we need to know what's going on. Our communications have been lit up like fireworks on Interdependence Day. If there is any way we can help people and their parrots, you know you can count on me."

Ronnie's phone gave off a new parrot call, signaling he'd been added to a new networking group, the CDIT. "Wow, that was quick. Oh my god! The infection is here."

"Yup."

"Not just in parrots, but in people."

"Yup."

Ronnie said, "Is it too early to start drinking?"

"You and me both. Why don't you go down to the cafeteria or have something droned in? Cincinnati's been all vegan for several years, so the restaurants are good."

"I know. I grew up near here," said Ronnie.

"I forgot," he said, never looking up from the back-up paperwork that came with the chip data from PACT. "Great, I see you've listed health attributes of each bird and causes for each death. There's a few samples without much information, but," he said under his breath, "I know nothing. I know nothing." He grinned at Ronnie in the collusion, ramping up the intensity of the moment.

"We have duplicates back at PACT, but if you have any sample volume leftover, we'd like to have it returned."

"You betcha, but probably not today. We might need to repeat tests or do different ones."

While in the cafeteria, Ronnie reviewed the regional CDIT reports and communications and summaries from the Australasia originating CDIT. He read faster, then read it again. He had to get back now. He nearly ran to Bill's lab.

"Hey, Bill, I need to head back. Can you send me the results?"

"Oh sure. Your sample code numbers begin with PCT."

"One more thing, Bill, have you worked with parrots before?"

"No. Why?"

"Because if you had, you'd be a lot more upset than you are."

"Believe me, I'm none too happy. But, strangely enough, there's a thrill to it. This is what I trained for."

"Well, I didn't train for it, but I've gotten a lot of practice dealing with one disaster after another with our birds. And I'm telling you, practice doesn't make perfect. It just pisses me off."

"Sure, I get it. Sorry this is so tough. If you or any others need support, they've already staffed counselors and social scientists on the CDIT. It's standard practice because the toll disease outbreaks, real or imagined, take on the human psyche is well documented."

"Not to mention the wildlife involved. I gotta go!"

"Okay. PCT. Don't forget."

Ronnie was halfway home when the results came in. If he'd had the wheel, the car would have crashed. As it was, he suddenly felt so sick that he barely had time to open the trash compacter before he vomited. Taking deep breaths, he focused on the passing scenery, and saw a flock of lorikeets perched on an old telephone wire. That snapped him out of his shock enough to call an emergency meeting of PACT. The car continued down the road, oblivious to the tumult in its occupant.

"Hello, Ronnie. Do you have results yet?" asked Kabuki.

"Yes," he croaked.

"Are you all right?"

"No, I'm not, and neither are we."

Kasuku frowned, "I see."

"I'm sending the results now."

"They're still coded. Can you decipher them?" asked Ayoka.

Ronnie said, "Here's the short of it. We've got the parrot prion throughout the sanctuary."

"It's a mix of birds from all over the world, so we often see emerging diseases come up. That's why we kept the suns and the Carolinas strictly separated," said Ayoka.

"Yeah, but it didn't work."

"What didn't work?"

"It's in the suns and the Carolinas."

"But how?" asked Kasuku. "We were so careful. We went to Guyana to get breeding and genetic stock from wild sun parakeets so the Carolinas would never be exposed to suns from the captive trade."

"Maybe it happened with the first generation of sun parakeets. They came from Guyana with the prion in their system and we didn't know to test for it. Our modified germ cells using CRISPR to turn the sun parakeet genome as much as possible into a Carolina genome were clear of the prion. But we injected these germ cells into a recently laid sun egg, so maybe the sun passed on the prions through the egg," said Ayoka.

"Or through exposure to the suns we used as parents so that the first generation of Carolina parakeets were raised by birds, not by humans."

"I don't know how it happened, but it did. And there's more bad news," said Ronnie.

"How can anything be worse than that?"

Ronnie said, "Easy for you to say. I tested positive, too. And so did thousands of parrot people all over the world, many of whom are sick, and many of whom are asymptomatic."

"Which are you?" asked Jessie, swallowing a sob.

"I haven't been feeling well, but I thought it was depression and age. I'll get it checked out. They have developed a protocol for triaging symptoms and recommending a battery of diagnostic tests. I'll let you know."

"I hate to be the one to say this, but I don't see how we can release Carolinas if they are carriers of disease. Even if we could afford to start over, what chance do we have of insuring a clean blood line?" Jimmy's stern face belied his training as a litigator.

"But if all parrots have it, what harm is there?" asked Jessie.

"Because we don't have natural parrots in the USA. Some people might think we have a chance of eradication here," said Ayoka.

"That's preposterous! There are thousands of naturalized parrots in the majority of states that have been breeding for decades," Ronnie argued.

"I'm sorry, what does naturalized mean?" asked Jimmy.

"It means that the parrots were brought here from their native homes without choice because of the parrot trade and were released or escaped. The have adapted to the USA and established populations. In other words, the USA is now their home," Ronnie replied.

"That argument doesn't hold political weight. Just because people or other species were forcibly migrated due to economics, violence, or climate change, the USA has periodically said they must go, no matter the consequences to individuals and families," said Jimmy.

"But to get rid of the disease would mean getting rid of all the parrots. All those that escaped long ago and established stable populations, and the more recent ones released during this scare, and all those in captivity – here even." Jessie's voice trailed off.

"Hey, let's not go there, we don't know how this is going to play out," warned Ayoka.

Ronnie thought he knew how it was going to play out. They'd kill them all.

Chapter 19
South Australia

"Hey, you guys, I really appreciate the protection, but my arms are getting tired," Kendi said to Rak and three other scarlets clinging to her as she walked up the hill to get her messages. Ketura and Lapta walked in front of her, each with a small, flapping macaw on their heads. They were Rak's fledglings, who Kendi was learning had names that sounded like Chrreeeet and Rrrrret. Orlin and Cherik had gone ahead to make sure the way was clear. Kendi had long learned the name of Cherik, Rak's steadfast mate.

She still couldn't believe how Lucero and the military had backed away from a confrontation after the vote, but she didn't trust them not to do something clandestine. Despite her general unease, Kendi appreciated that she felt like they were two families going for a leisurely Sunday afternoon stroll and flight.

As she neared the hill and turned towards Nicaragua, the border clearly distinguishable by the sudden lack of trees on the other side of Honduras, her phone spewed all kinds of noises. She knew she should have expected work to have accumulated, but not thousands of flagged messages. When her phone chirped, she knew it was Aria.

"Oh, Kendi, I'm so glad I got you. I've been calling and calling, and left a ton of messages."

"It's been crazy here. We had so many visitors that I couldn't get away."

"I saw the video. And then heard how you were voted not only president of the new independent nation, but you're also the Mama Guara Tara of all your people, not just your village. I am so proud of you! And jealous. All our parrots in New Zealand just left, while yours flocked to you."

"Why did they do that?"

"Some of my colleagues have been analyzing their communication right before they left, and it looks like they were angry and fearful. They knew there was trouble and planned to "not see" and "not be seen.""

"What trouble?"

"Oh right, you haven't been following the news. Parrot Prion Disease Syndrome has upset people, and some are taking it out on parrots."

"But it's only in New Zealand and Australia, right?"

"No, we've found it in other places, and it could be where you are. That's why I'm calling. Be careful around the birds. You and the birds must be tested."

Kendi looked up with incredulity at the four children rolling in the savannah grass. "These parrots would never do anything to hurt us. I've never even been bitten. If there is a chance that the disease moves from parrots to people, it's probably too late anyway. You know how closely we live with them here."

"Kendi, I've got the prion, and I may be sick. You could have it, too. So for me, please get tested."

"Oh no, Aria, how can that be?"

"The prion seems to have a stronger predilection for people

who've been around parrots, but not everyone gets sick, or they haven't developed the disease yet. There's much we don't know. I'm part of the CDIT team, and we arranged for a PMCA reader and test kits to be sent to Kirtira, along with a med tech from Tegucigalpa who knows the equipment."

"This is serious, Aria."

"It is. Have you or any others shown any symptoms, like loss of balance? Behavioral or personality changes? Sudden dementia?"

Kendi paused, and let the reality rise from her subconscious, finally giving it space. "Yes, we've had some sick families. There's been a rumor for a while that keeping parrots or poaching them is bad for you. The older poachers have all died in the last years."

"How did they die?"

"They either fell from trees or *fue loco*, or both."

"Now I really am worried. Can you do something today? For me?"

"Yes, of course. What do I need to do?"

"I've sent the protocol for collecting samples to your inbox. We need blood from your family and others, as well as from each species of parrot. Also, could you collect some samples from around the flight cages and the village and forest?" Aria didn't say why they needed environmental samples. This was a theory her team was working on.

"Aria, I need to go if I'm going to get this done today. But first, how are you?"

"I'm surrounded by people I love and who love me. I am fine, no matter what happens."

"It's the same for me here, so don't worry."

Just then Rak, perhaps recognizing Aria's voice, moved into

199

the view of the vid screen, and squawked, "Grauk."

"Oh hello, Rak, it's good to see you too. I'll leave you now. It looks like you're in good wings."

"*Yamni was.*"

"*Kaiki was.*"

Aria turned from the alcove near the living quarters and looked out over the laboratory. In the late evening, people were still working with impassioned attention, while the six lab live-ins had moved into a calmer routine, as much as possible with the potential for a pandemic under their microscopes. Aria knew this was the scene all over the world and found solace in knowing they weren't solely responsible for the research. They still had their environmental sample investigation headed by Jule. Nikau, Tiago, and Baraka were busy conducting and coordinating pathology analyses of parrot neurological tissues, mostly from brains. They still had found no signs of the prion disease in parrots. They hadn't unlocked what the prion was doing in parrots and how it got from them to humans. That was the key.

Nikau looked up at Aria with concern in his eyes. "How are you feeling?"

"Fine. Just a little tired. I might actually get a full night's sleep tonight."

"Only because I tested negative," he said and smiled. "I'll be glad when we discover how humans get the prion so we can pick up where we almost got started."

"Me too. See you in the morning."

"Wait, Aria. I need to talk to you all now," said Daku.

"What's up?"

"You've been tracking Typhoon Diwa, right?"

She said, "Yes, but not a lot. We seem to have other more

200

important things to concentrate on."

"Maybe not now. Diwa has increased forward speed and wind speed."

"But it's not headed here, or at least the last I saw."

"As of now, but typhoons are tricky here. They can be jumpy, and Diwa is moving extremely fast.

"You said earlier this is a cyclone-proof smart building," said Nikau.

Daku said, "It is, but rated to category 5, like our downtown flood structures. Diwa is growing stronger and could be south Australia's first category 6."

"Suddenly I don't feel so tired," said Aria, yawning in exhaustion despite the news. "I want to get as much done as possible in case the typhoon comes this way. Everyone can decide for themselves."

"If it comes to it," Helga asked, "do you have generators?"

"Yes," said Daku, "we're set up with huge batteries and solar panels too. We also have a top-story storm shelter because storm surges can get wicked here."

"So, we can work all the way through the storm?" Helga pressed.

"Technically, yes. That goal was in the architects' planning, that we would be able to address diseases even under the worst climatic situation."

"I'm staying," said Helga.

"Me too," said Nikau and Jule together, with Tiago and Baraka echoing them a split second later.

Daku said, "I will do a check on the building. The generators have been giving us a little trouble."

"Hey, before you go, Daku," Jule called across the room,

"how are your family and others around Adelaide?"

"My immediate family was never around parrots, but people are scared. We have so many parrots in Australia. They're everywhere. Some fringe groups are threatening to kill them all, or at least the urban populations."

"No way! The parrots were here first!" said Jule.

"Many think like you do, but some act rashly when they're afraid. And their anxiety is ramped up even more with a major storm in the area. I've got to go," said Daku, leaving the lab.

"So much for my good night's sleep," Aria grumbled to Nikau, reaching for a cup of coffee with one hand and swiping through the latest results with the other. The others returned their work, napping when they could until late into the night. That's how Aria and others happened to be in the lab when the results came in from other places in the world.

"Oh no, the Carolina parakeets have it! How did it get to North America from New Zealand?" asked Jule.

"I have a theory," said Tiago. "Europe has a strong aviculture culture, and private collections have been adding keas for decades."

"Okay, that's how it got to Europe. And then with the parrot trade it spread maybe to Africa, and that might be how Jule, Helga, and Baraka were exposed. But how did it cross the ocean? And come to think about it, how did you get it? Did you ever work in Europe with parrots?" said Aria.

"I did not," said Tiago, "but I handle a lot of parrot tissues from all over the world. Once I nicked my gloved finger with a scalpel during a necropsy."

"Okay, that's you, and I'm sorry. But how did it get to the wild parrots?" said Jule.

"Keas ended up in zoos in the Americas, too, but I think it came from another direction, or perhaps both. The prion is in Brazil and the spix macaws, too," he said pointing to results on the wall screen."

"Which were donated to Brazil from Europe after they went extinct in the wild as part of a reintroduction project," said Aria.

"Yes, collectors taketh and giveth away," said Jule, proud of her English, but not of her fellow European citizens.

"The project got a lot of criticism for risking introducing exotic diseases into the wild parrot population because, case in point, no matter how much you test, you can't rule out that something undetectable at that time is leaking through," said Helga.

"But nobody thought of testing for prion disease in those earlier days, especially since parrots don't get the disease and don't show symptoms," said Aria. "But even still, people should have been more careful because –"

Aria gasped at the screen, "It's in Honduras' parrots! But human results aren't in yet."

"So, it got there either from keas in zoos in the USA and then entered the imported parrots that established themselves in the wild and slowly moved south, or it came from Brazil and headed north. Could have originated in both places actually," said Tiago.

"The only place we haven't seen it is Asia," said Nikau.

"You spoke too soon. There's China's results. It's there too."

"Now how did it get to China?" asked Luther who holo-hovered nearby.

"I can answer that one," said Aria. "There's been a market for parrot eggs and chicks being smuggled out of wild populations to feed the international demand for years. The parrots in La Moskitia, Honduras, where my cousin Kendi lives, would have been long gone without their rangers protecting them from illegal trafficking and the pressure from international buyers.

"How are the results from Africa looking?"

"I contacted my colleagues there and they're testing in several countries," Baraka said. "That parrots have long been illegally traded between Europe and Africa points to a near certainty that it's there. And African greys still are smuggled all over the world."

"I don't think we have any choice but to recommend to each regional CDIT that they lock down all travel until we know how the prion is transmitted. They're all seeing the same results as we are, so I don't think it'll come as a surprise. Agreed?" said Luther, eyeing Helga as if in a dare, but Helga winked back.

He swiped his holo keyboard, sending out multiple messages, and he was correct. Other regions were not surprised because they'd seen a wave of red roll through the continents, as one after another country shut down. Breaking through the overall red were many pinpoints marking where people had tested positive. Circles indicated a high concentration of these outbreaks, and X's marked higher concentrations of people with elevated symptom indexes or diseases confirmed by brain tissue analysis, either post- or antemortem.

"That's the biggest, scariest tic-tac-toe board I've ever seen," whistled Nikau.

"A game rigged against whoever goes second," said Aria, looking at the others who full well knew what she meant: Parrots flew all over Earth millions of years before humans ever took their first step.

Chapter 20
South Australia

A few hours later, Nikau called to the team, "You better come watch this." He switched one of the screens to the new 24/7 PPDS Update channel.

The news commentator was saying, "And we are getting reports from several major locations in the world about potentially violent protests. People are calling for government parrot eradication programs and threatening to take action if the government doesn't do something. Counter-protests are further swelling the streets."

"Look," said Jule, "the unrest is almost exclusively located where parrots are not naturally present, such as Spain and other parts of Europe, the USA, Canada, China."

"They've always been considered throw-away birds. People took them from their homelands and then abandoned them. That's why there's so many parrot sanctuaries in those countries. You can't let them go outside," said Aria bitterly, "for instance, like we did with keas in New Zealand."

"Except they are letting parrots go!" said Nikau watching a clip of a flock of cockatoos perched on the Eifel tower.

Nikau, Aria, and Jule were beeped alerts at the same time.

Nikau said, "The US is calling for unconditional solidarity for people to protect parrots wherever they are."

"It's so hard to be stuck in the lab. I feel like we need to get out there and do more," said Aria.

"The best thing we can do is figure out this disease," said Helga. "We have reports of people with no history with parrots but they're testing positive. Prions should not be so transmissible."

"I know, I know," said Aria. "I just feel that so much is at stake and it's all slipping away.

Reading her holo-pad on her smart watch, Jule said, "I think I know why people are testing positive." She touched her watch band and her results flipped up on the board. A map of the world emerged showing various colors, with New Zealand and Australia beaming the darkest red.

"What are we looking at?" asked Tiago, staring at Brazil tinged with orange, especially compared to Antarctica, all white.

"The colors indicate environmental samples that tested positive for PrK," said Jule.

"So, it's nearly everywhere," said Aria and slumped.

Luther holoed in, looking like he'd slept in his clothes. Aria was envious that he got to sleep.

"What does it mean?" said a surveillance and public health rep who appeared with Luther.

"In means that PrK is in soil, pastures, crops, and, look, even water," said Jule.

"I get that, but what does it mean for the world?" the holo asked. So many people were involved that the Adelaide team had lost track of who was there.

"It means we're fucked," said Helga, stopping the

conversation.   Everyone stared at her.   "Excuse my unprofessionalism, but this means we have no chance to eradicate PrK because if it's like other prions, it's long lasting and hard to eradicate in the environment, let alone in parrots."

"But we don't know if people contract the disease from environmental samples, at least not yet, right?" asked Luther.

"Other mammals contract similar prion diseases from ingesting contaminated forage, so I don't see why we can't either," said Aria.

"And the incidence of asymptomatic cases correlates with the environmental samples," said Jule, merging two maps into one.

"In other words, though too early to say definitively, if it's in the environment it gets into humans?" asked a holo.

"Yeah, like Helga said. It's the aparrotclypse for sure!" said Nikau, offering a weak moment of humor.

"Maybe. But we're missing something. How come we don't have more sick people? Those showing symptoms are only a small subset of those testing positive and of those who have been around parrots or in areas of high environmental contamination," Luther said as he highlighted various maps.

"Either the answer is because of some other complex interaction with some other factors that will take great effort to discover, or it's so simple it would bite us on the nose if we were any closer to figuring it out," said Jule, again showing her prowess of English idioms.

"Hey, you might be on to something," Helga said as she crunched her eyes and pursed her lips.

"What?" several voices asked.

"Aria, have you ever been bitten by a parrot?"

"Sure, plenty of times, especially when I was a kid working with keas. They can be nippy."

"Jule?"

"Yes, but it never broke the skin."

"Tiago?"

"No, but remember I cut myself once working with dead parrot tissues."

"Baraka?"

"Oh, yes. Rescuing African greys from poachers was often an emergency situation to get them unpacked from the cages they were stuffed in. The birds were so scared, they'd bite anything."

"I myself have had my fair share of bites," said Helga. "Nikau?"

"Never been bitten or exposed to parrot tissues."

"Okay, you are a small sample, but I think I see what you're getting at," said Luther. "We know that other prion diseases can be transmitted through exposure to contaminated tissues or surgical instruments, but why wouldn't humans get it from ingestion?"

"Maybe the digestive process is somehow protective, maybe impacting the protein salt bridge," suggested Aria.

"Let's broaden our sampling, shall we?" said Luther. "While we've been talking, I used MASCD to add questions about bites and blood exposure. Bob, access Carol and ask her to check all surveys that mention parrot bites or blood exposure, and project the results, which amazingly are already coming in."

"Wow, and I thought I was glued to this app," said Nikau

"Carol, show us any correlation between parrot bite or parrot blood and tissue exposure and the symptom index," said

Luther.

Carol recited, "Insufficient data to say with any confidence, but the deviations are increasingly narrowing as more information is processed. The correlation coefficient is trending away from zero, but is still not very high."

"What about the reverse?" offered Helga.

"Carol, compare those who have no bite or blood exposure and are asymptomatic." Luther said.

"Insufficient data to say with any confidence, but the deviations are increasingly narrowing as more information is processed. The correlation coefficient is trending away from zero toward one."

"So maybe those who aren't bitten don't have the disease?" asked Luther.

"Double negatives drive me crazy." Nikau shook his head.

"Carol, of those showing the highest symptom index, how many have not been bitten or had blood exposure?" Aria asked.

"None," said Carol.

The room jumped at the sound of a loud crash.

"Bob, project external building cameras on wall screens," said Daku through audio. "Sorry I'm not there in holoperson or otherwise. The building alert just woke me."

On the screen a twenty-meter tree had fallen onto the building.

"The building woke you up for this?" asked Nikau.

"No, it woke me because Diwa just made a sudden turn and intensified. The eye is coming straight for Adelaide as a Category Six-plus. It's huge and you couldn't outrun it even if you tried. It might change course and follow you wherever you go."

They'd been so busy they missed the latest reports from the

International Typhoon Tracker. They saw a red line coming straight at them and then heading back out to sea, on course for New Zealand.

Jule gasped. "It's going to be here in a couple of hours!"

"Finish what you're working on. Make sure that all data is backed up in several places and servers in the cloud. Then move to the upper storm shelter section of the building," said Daku. Then, "Uh oh."

"What now?" asked Nikau.

"The building is telling me that the generators aren't functioning. The building won't be at full capacity. Even more reason to clear out as soon as you can," urged Daku.

The group began to disperse. "We need to see to patients." "I need to implement emergency protocols." "They're going to need our help monitoring evacuations." "We need to end this meeting."

"But what do we tell the world? This storm could shut us down for hours. In that time thousands of parrots could be killed, and as many people harmed in the protests," said Aria.

"She's right, we need a statement to go out now before everything shuts down. I just made a break-out room where we can craft a new public alert. We should say that it appears people do not transmit the disease to each other, nor do we contract the disease from a contaminated environment. And parrots do not pose a risk if you do not get bit or exposed to their blood. Did I sum that up alright?" asked Luther.

"It is a zombie disease!" said Nikau.

"Except that you may contract it from living with parrots in the home, and that parrots do not have any neurological symptoms or brain changes," said Aria.

"Well, that might not be the case," said Tiago.

"He could be right," Baraka began but stopped. "Hey, look at the trees. They're full of parrots! And more are coming in!" Everyone turned to the building cameras.

"We planted windbreak trees that wouldn't cause damage if the winds felled them, and they have lots of leaves to break the wind. Cockatoos and some other parrots have been using them for roost sites. I guess they were surprised by the typhoon, too, and didn't move to a more protected area," said Daku.

"If one tree fell when the typhoon isn't even here yet, they could all die!" said Aria.

Nikau looked at her, admiring her unwavering championship of parrots.

"They're deeply rooted trees. Maybe that tree was diseased," said Daku.

"I hope the typhoon slows down and takes another turn. Typhoons have a long history of being hard on birdlife," said Jule.

"And on humans. Let's get moving," ordered Luther, harsher than he meant. "We'll see you on the other side of this thing. Stay safe."

"Hey look," said Jule. "It's PACT on the news. Helga and I spent time there a few years ago. It's under attack! Wow, hundreds of people carrying guns and wearing masks. I hope Ronnie and the others are okay."

Helga could see they were not okay. The cameras zoomed in on a large cockatoo flying around with a human eye in his beak. Gunfire erupted and someone screamed just as the lab went dark.

Chapter 21
Kentucky, USA

The morning before the lab team watched the video and even before the video was recorded, Ronnie had a premonition. He knew things were far from okay when again he woke feeling terrible. He didn't know if the cause was the parrot prion, because he had so many reasons to feel bad. The news yesterday about PPDS had only gotten worse every hour, and he feared for the birds' lives. If the PACT board didn't take action to preserve public safety, the vigilantes would. He was particularly worried about the RedDeaders, who styled themselves after an old video game of a similar name. The game was set in a time of American decline, and gamers earned points if they could shoot all the rare Carolina parakeets. The internet was flooded with regional groups, and the FBI had called PACT to warn them of an active group in Cincinnati. So serious was the FBI taking the threat that an agent had visited the campus to review their security protocols. The sheriff assigned extra patrol cars and drones to the area.

Ronnie didn't see a way out of this mess, and so he did what he always did when he had problems: he fed the birds and talked to them. He hoped Hercules would offer some wisdom, as he headed to the cockatoos' building. He had tweaked the sunrise protocol on the building's parameters so the birds would have some normalcy before he entered and turned on the lights. He was way early and didn't want to disturb the birds and trigger the more anxious ones. He thought how warm and still the pre-dawn air felt. Always calm before the storm he worried, entering the building and heading directly to Hercules. That led him on a train of thought about how some species of birds were known to sense a storm system days ahead and evacuate out of harm's way. He stopped outside of Hercules' flight, and said in jest, "Hey, Herc, are you up to flying the hell away from here?"

He heard himself and realized that was the answer, not a great one, but it could work. The birds could just leave. It was a warm winter, more food trees had been planted, and stands of old trees in the hallows and along the ridges of this historical Kentucky farmland, on the southern side of the Ohio River, might be ideal. They wouldn't all survive, but some might and that was better than none, he reasoned. After the security lock scanned his retina and popped the lock, he entered the flight, pausing for Hercules to signal that it was okay to enter all the way. He leaned back to throw his jacket over the camera just as Hercules broke the avian silence, "Chenerrech!" Startled, Ronnie missed and his jacket fell on the floor. He didn't notice, so intent was he on the flock before him, stretching their wings, preening, not displaying any repetitive behaviors.

"Looks like all of you woke up on the right side of the perch. I didn't, so I'm just going to sit here on this sawed-off trunk and rest for a bit. Is that okay?" In response Hercules bobbed his head and flew down to a lower perch where he was eye level with Ronnie. He tilted his head as Ronnie continued.

"No seriously, Herc, do you think the plan would work? I

could open all the flights and the outer door, and then you all could hide in the trees until this problem passes. We could put out food until you all got used to foraging on your own and summer came around. But I don't know if I should, Herc. I'd hate to be the cause of spreading the parrot prion even more. But you aren't dangerous, are you? If people would learn to just leave parrots alone, I think they'd be safe, and you all certainly would." Ronnie looked up into Herc's eyes and saw a depth of understanding and intent. Maybe Herc didn't understand everything, he thought, but he did seem to grok the situation.

"Okay, deal then? Let's do this!"

Ronnie stood up, but the room spun and he crashed to the floor, hitting his head on some fallen toys that had been chewed lose from their usual hanging locations. Herc's crest went up, as did several others, and their wings quickly extended, ready to fly from whatever had felled the human.

"Guess I stood up too quick," said Ronnie. His hand went to his head and came back red. "I probably have PPDS with loss of balance, I lost my beloved Eddie, and I'm about to lose my life's work. But hey, Herc, other than that, don't worry, I'm okay." Just then a searing pain went down his arm to his bloodied hand that was shaking.

"Oh shit, let me amend the list to add a heart attack. And a bad one, Herc." His words escaped through a tight grimace.

Herc flew down to the floor, walked up to Ronnie, and began peeping like a chick. He reached out to Hercules' bowed head and stroked the bird who leaned into Ronnie with his whole body. "Herc, you know, it wasn't just Eddie. You've been the love of my life as well, and you, too," he said to the other birds flying down to join Hercules in a human-parrot group hug.

215

The pain began to recede, but so did his field of view that narrowed to Hercules.

"I'm not going to make it, Herc, so it's all up to you." He weakly lifted his hand to his eye. "You know what you have to do, don't you, buddy?"

Herc clucked harshly, like a deep human groan in utmost grief, and then began peeping. Ronnie's hand fell as he said his last words, "Hurry. Fly free." Herc's peeping faded with Ronnie's heartbeat.

Herc let out a long cry, "Keeeensh," an avian wail for the ages. The others added their cries. Looking back at hard eye, he saw red, which made him pause, knowing he was being watched. He shook his head as if throwing off a burden. He leaned closer to Ronnie's still face and with careful but hurried tearing, he soon had Ronnie's parting gift in his beak. He flew to the scanner and lowered the eye at the level he had seen the controllers do thousands of times, and the door popped open.

"Cheneerrech, fly with me!" he called over his shoulder. He flew to the flight across the aisle. He heard wings behind him and knew that not all would brave the sudden change in circumstances, and some couldn't fly. But he didn't pause because first light was nearly upon him. With Ronnie's gift, he had the power of a controller. He opened one flight door after another. When every flight was open and flying and walking parrots were everywhere, he said "Flee fast and fly hard! To the Freeforest!" He opened the outside door and disappeared.

He flew to the tree canopy, where he could see the many noforest spaces below him. His responsibility pulled him back down to Earth as he flew directly to the long-tail noforest, repeating his use of Ronnie's seeing-gift to open doors, freeing the captives, and then the next noforest, and the next. He thought he had freed all the birds and was headed back to the safety of the canopy when he saw a group of noforests set apart from the others. He flew to one of the isolated noforests, opened that door and entered into a forest-no forest, adorned with birds the color of the first light. They all turned, as if one, and cried, "Sakfreet!" An alarm and contact call mixed together.

He flew around looking for the hard eyes that would react to Ronnie's gift. His eyes adjusted to make out subtle changes in the forest-noforest, and found the retinal scanner buried in a bush. The nano-forest started to break up in patches. At first the parakeets didn't move, though some leaned into the openings. "Chennerrech, fly with me!" They recognized his sound from the many nights of drumming and dancing. "Be the Firstbirds you were hatched to be!"

With that, it was as if the sun had hatched hundreds of children who exploded in flight to the door and out of the building. He flew with them, the color of the moon mixed with the sun. "Fly free to the trees!" he urged them as he veered off to free the sun birds from the last noforests.

When he finished and was finally heading into the trees, he looked down and saw Controller Two looking up at him, his nobeak agape, his loving heart pure *agape*. Jessie fell to his knees, sobbing for the drab ravaged landscape of his mind that had been restored with the beauty of the many suns, moons, stars, and rainbows that had come to Earth to roost at last.

Chapter 22
South Island, New Zealand

Donika gave up trying to reach Aria and was as frantic as she'd ever been. Her daughter was in the path of the storm's obliteration, which was heading toward Donika to do the same. Donika thought how like-mother like-daughter they were. They shared everything: storms, PPDS in those they loved but not in themselves, and, no PrK, though apparently having PrK didn't mean you'd develop the disease.

But for some reason, Isaac had. And he was in a hospital, alone. She was alone too, and she was tired of it. She had friends and family, but she realized that if she excluded even one being from having inherent worth and dignity, it was she who was alone. If not everyone was beloved, then no one was.

"Now I'm sounding like Aria's Lapatistas, she said aloud. "To hell with quarantine and evacuation, I'm going to get Isaac and bring him home."

She reached Dr. Jennings who said he would meet her at the hospital to spring Isaac. With the latest PPDS update, quarantine might be lifted, maybe soon, as the prion was proving not to be contagious between humans.

She chafed at having to put on the bio-PPE outside Isaac's isolation wing, suddenly anxious to see him as soon as possible.

She cringed when she realized that she felt like she had when visiting Kaleb in his last days in isolation. She had stepped out of Kaleb's room for coffee, and when she hurried back, a team of doctors had encircled him, trying to resuscitate him. But the machines didn't lie. Kaleb had flat-lined without her saying goodbye. Time slowed down as she dropped her coffee, its slow-motion splatter seared into her memory.

But this time, only one other person was in the room with Isaac, Luther. "Donika," Isaac said and beamed. "I hear you're breaking me out. I just hope it's to free me, and not to take justice into your own hands." He raised an eyebrow.

"You have even more bandages than you had the last time I saw you." She ignored his comment. His head looked like it was wrapped in a turban.

Isaac looked to Luther and nodded his approval to continue.

"I was just telling Isaac about his brain biopsy results," said Luther.

"You gave permission for that?"

"Yeah, unlike me to be so self-sacrificing?"

"Well, yes."

"We're glad that he did because we learned so much. He has all the changes typical of a prion disease that's been incubating for decades," said Luther.

"But I thought that once people showed symptoms, they lapsed into a syndrome that led to death within months, or years, not decades."

"Maybe it hits people differently, but Isaac has had this a long time, including the symptoms. We did a thorough work-up, as you know. He is in many ways our Patient 0."

"What are you telling me?" Donika asked bewildered.

"He's exhibited aberrant or uncontrolled behavior patterns for a long time, likely due to the brain changes caused by the abnormal prion replication cluttering his brain."

"Look, Donika, when I told Aria I didn't remember what Kaleb and I fought about in medical school, I haven't been able to remember for decades. Hell, even the day after we fought, I wasn't sure what happened. And after that I just couldn't cut the academic rigor of school, and I left. Kaleb and I never talked about it again. I'm not asking you to forgive me, or saying that I don't take full responsibility for what happened, but I think it's important for our family history, and for you, and Aria, and those that will one day call us their ancestors to know. I'm sorry, Donika."

"Oh, Isaac, I've been such a *pendeja*. I figured someone had to be blamed for all the pain and loss, and you were such an easy target."

Donika asked, "Will you come home with me?" just as Isaac asked, "Can I go home now?"

Isaac reached for Donika, and she took his hand. Luther's eyes seemed a little glassy when he said, "You're all set. I've signed him out. Just follow the same home quarantine protocols we set up for you and Callum."

"Which I just broke by coming here."

"That's okay, we're going to have to move a lot of people out of here if Diwa continues on her current course. You'd be doing us a favor to take him home."

A nurse walked into the room with a wheelchair and said, "A huge favor. Believe me!"

"I don't need a damn wheelchair! I ain't dead yet. But maybe soon," Isaac's voice faded to a whisper as he reluctantly climbed into the wheelchair.

Donika nodded in solidarity with the nurse as she wheeled Isaac toward the front door.

Isaac said, "Speaking of favors, I have a big one to ask, Donika."

"Indeed?" she said, knowing Isaac never asked for help.

"I need to talk to the keas, one in particular, if she's still alive."

"We don't know where the keas are. They disappeared after the one you shot escaped from Kowhai. As we've lost drones over a large area we can't pinpoint where they are exactly. It appears they have sent out sentinel birds to protect their home base."

"I think I know where they are. I'll need help getting to them."

"We've checked all the usual places, and there's no sign of them.

"Did you check the wilding conifer grove near dad's old hunting cabin?"

"No. Why do you think they're there?"

"Because granddad told me he used to go hunting up in that area with his father, and he heard stories about how keas would roost in the radiata pines, until the keas were all shot or scared away by hunters."

"The radiatas are considered trash trees that keas don't like. Why would they go to a place where others had been killed?"

"Because they're crafty birds. Will you drive me there?"

"When?"

"Now?"

"What's so urgent? Especially given your condition and a typhoon on its way?"

"I don't know how much longer I'll be able to do this, even with help. And I have more wrongs to right. We have to go to my place anyway to pick up some clothes and check on my ranch hands. They told me they repaired the ATV. You can drive it up the old logging road."

"But if the weather turns bad, we'll be in a world of hurt."

"Don't make me beg, Donika," he said reaching for her hand. "I need to do this."

"Let me make some calls to arrange for Callum's care and get some supplies in case we get stuck up there. I always enjoy an adventure, even stupid ones."

"Spoken like a true Roberts and Lacuth!"

A few hours later they were headed up and out of the valley, alone on the land.

Above, scouting for the clan, Chiznek screeched, "The baldskins are coming!" He flew high and cried loud, spreading the message to those foraging far from the old home. Chiznek thought he had enough time to get to the old home before the baldskins if he flew fast and hard.

He arrived, breathing rapidly, not too subtly landing in the oldest tree about midway up. He knew that Turagg would be there because that's where they'd taken Maitita, who all called grandmother. She couldn't fly far and high to go over the mountains to hide in the remotest areas, so they'd carried her to the old home. She cried when they arrived, unsure if it was from pain or memory. She couldn't perch in a tree very well, but there was a hard deadtree floor that the nonwingeds had built in the tree years ago. They brought moss and leaves, making grandmother as comfortable as they could.

Turagg greeted him, "Rest your feathers, young one, and tell us what you saw."

He didn't know he was quivering, and shame sleeked him down.

"Rockboy is coming on his fourroundfeet, and with him is Good-helper. They're coming to kill us. We must go!"

Just then Bruka bustled through the thickly set branches. "No, we must attack. What worked once before will once again. Your young ones are hungry, Turagg. Let's sound a blood and beauty call and meet them before they come here to threaten the oldest, the youngest, and those who were just liberated and fly poorly."

Turagg had chosen this place for the pine branches that were thick, and where they could hide from the nonwingeds. Here was protection from the humans, and the storm, he sensed.

"Did you see any kill-sticks?"

"No," said Chiznek.

"And there were only two of them?"

"Yes."

"And one is Good-helper?"

"Yes," answered Chiznek, glad to be calmer and proud of his stoic scout reporting.

"I don't know why she would be with Rockboy," said Turagg.

Bruka, said, "She has turned. A feather promise means nothing to the baldskins."

"She saved me and cared for me," said Junptra." I won't see her harmed."

"She must be coming for a reason, but why with Rockboy?"

"If the nonwingeds discover us here, all is lost," warned Bruka.

"But they already know we're here," said Maitita rolling from her side to stand on her one leg. "They come to meet with us, and meet with them we will."

"But, Grandmother, Rockboy is the one who hurt you. And it's the nonwingeds who killed your loves and your chicks," said flustered Chiznek, out of respect avoiding the pejorative 'baldskins' when talking to an old one.

"You're young yet and haven't learned that we must face our past and the dark side within us all to make the best choices. Will we become the killers that the nonwingeds are? Will we be the destroyer of trees and the captors of the many?"

"You speak wisely," said Turagg, "but let's act wisely as well. Take all who can fly now to the higher treehome, Chiznek and Bruka. I'll stay with Grandmother and learn their intent."

"As will I," said Junptra.

"No, you must take our three and flee."

Junptra said, "I will not and cannot. My wings are weak still, as is my heart. I can't bear to be so far from you. If there is danger, we face it together."

"And our children?"

"They're the children of the future. Let them be a part of what's to come."

"Yes, Papa, we want to be with you and Mama," said the oldest, Crnac, and the younger two nodded.

"Okay, but stay in the thickest part of the branches. Remember how I showed you to fly low in the trees to escape hunters." Turning to the scouts, he said, "Hurry and tell the others they're free to flee or stay. They're coming!"

The noise of the fourroundfeet could be heard echoing up from the valley. Turagg could see high flying keas heading their way, staying out of kill-stick range, in blood and beauty formation.

Grandmother began preening her unruly feathers that had grown astray from so much sitting and age. She was prepared to look Rockboy in the eye after all these years. He would see her strength that he couldn't kill. She tucked in the middle wing feathers, but they sprang out again as Good-helper and Rockboy arrived.

Good-helper got out of the fourroundfeet and helped Rockboy take a few steps toward them.

Donika had seen the keas flying parallel to them up the valley. She suspected others had landed deep in the high branches.

"Do you see them?" she asked Isaac.

"No, but I feel them. Don't you?"

Donika held still, her ears clearing from the jarring road and the engine. Though electric, it was still louder than the silence that settled over the cabin clearing.

"You're right. They're here. I didn't know you have the kea-sight." She turned towards him, as if seeing him for the first time. "Just like Maggie –"

"I've kept it hidden. I thought that part of me was dead. I sure tried to kill it, sometimes by killing those that stirred it in me. But lying in the hospital I felt my blood rousing, like I was a kea flying here. I am sorry," he whispered to Donika, then stepped away.

"I am sorry!" he said louder into the trees. "I am sorry!" he shouted as he turned in a circle to address every tree, and then fell against the ATV and sank to the ground. When Donika rushed to him, he said, "No, the guilt is mine alone to bear."

"It's not. Those days are gone. We face the past and the

future together."

He let her help him stand, then staggered a few feet toward the largest tree.

"Old one, are you there? I am sorry!"

Grandmother turned towards Turagg. "He, like me, needs help to move. Walk me out so we might know each other again. Perhaps for the first time."

Isaac saw two keas emerge from the green. He sensed many eyes on him. He said, "When I saw you all those years ago, flying free along the mountain ridges following Mom, I knew the love and connection she had with you. I hated you for what I dared not have myself. I hated myself. I was in silent rage when I waited for you at the spring. You sensed my intent and tried to fly away. I threw the stone. I caused your blood to fall from the sky into my eyes. I have seen your blood and your beauty. It's been within me ever since and always will be. I'm sorry I caused you a lifetime of pain. I dedicate my remaining time on Earth to you and yours. The beauty you are is what I do." Isaac bowed.

Donika echoed, "And so do I."

In the trees, Grandmother lowered herself onto the branch, and bowing her head, called down to them, "Sooodoi."

"Did she say, 'So do I'?" Donika said.

"She did," said Isaac as he wept, finally washing away the blood that had fallen long ago.

Chapter 23
South Australia

"Jule, would you do me a favor and take these reagents and plates up to the storm room? I'll be right up," said Aria.

"Watch your step. The emergency lights are running on the solar batteries and aren't very bright."

"Did the lights have to be red? For my part, I've seen too much red," said Nikau, heading for the stairs.

"This better be our last trip up," said Aria, noting the water seeping under the door. "So much for it being a typhoon-proof building."

"I grabbed some mattresses for everyone in case we're stuck upstairs. I found a manual about how to work this smart building," said Tiago. "Helga's up top studying it now."

"I got some snacks from the kitchen," said Baraka, nearly dropping his armload when a loud crash from outside shook them.

"Was that the building shaking?" asked Baraka. Without the wall screens they could only guess what destruction the typhoon was doing. The 6G network was down, and even satellite signals couldn't penetrate the massive storm. The flooding water hurried them upstairs, as did Helga's command, "Get in here now! I have to close the storm doors to the lower level. I already closed the storm walls that protect the nano-transparent walls."

"What did it look like out there?" said Aria. It was her first time upstairs.

"I could see only a river of water blowing sideways, and blurry objects flying. I hate to think of what the birds are going through."

"And anyone else out there who couldn't evacuate," said Jule, thinking of Daku.

Aria plopped down on one of the mattresses in the center of the room. Others joined her as they opened snacks and listened to the storm. Helga stood in the corner, tinkering on a fold-out console.

"That's a hell of storm if we can hear it through storm walls," said Tiago.

Helga said, "I opened up an audio channel to the outside. This building comes with a backup reduced system that runs on batteries. It's even got a mini weather station."

"Cool," said Nikau, joining Helga in the corner. Then, "Not so cool," he said, seeing a measurement of one gust of wind at 300 km/hour and sustained winds at 220 km/hour.

"Can we tell where the eye is?" asked Jule.

"Let me check the barometric pressure," Nikau said, then whistled.

"Well, what is it?" asked Aria who grew up in typhoon country.

"890 and still falling."

"That jives with the typhoon tracker and means, based on the last reports, we haven't seen the worst of the storm yet," said Aria.

They fell into a long silence, listening to wind and water.

Nikau broke the silence to report 875 and falling, with sustained winds at 240.

"Nikau, why don't you come get something to eat and rest?" asked Aria.

"I'm working on something," he said, his eyes shifting from the console to his phone's holo keyboard.

Aria joined him. "Are you thinking of the birds out there?"

"Yea, we can't save everyone but maybe we can help them."

"How?" said Jule and stood.

"Oh no, Nikau, you aren't thinking what I think you are?" said Tiago as he stood.

"What?" said Helga.

Aria said, "I know what you're doing. You're waiting for the eye to be right over us."

"How will that help the birds?" asked Helga.

"Because there's no wind in the eye –" said Tiago.

"Ahh, and we can open up the storm and nano-walls," said Helga.

"And somehow we'll get the birds to join us in the storm room before the eye passes," added Jule.

"That sounds just crazy and impossible enough to be something we should try," said Baraka.

"867 and holding. Wind speed – almost none. We're in the eye!"

"Are we agreed to this plan, everyone? This is not without risk from the storm and PrK. We can't guarantee we won't get bites," warned Helga.

"Unconditional solidarity!" Jule said, placing her hand in the center and the others followed.

"Helga, make it so!" commanded Nikau with a grin.

The storm walls rose. It looked like they were in the ocean, with upper floors of the buildings and some trees poking through.

"Did the building come unmoored?" asked Tiago.

"No, the ocean came to us," said Aria, moving to the other side of the building. "The roost trees are still there! They were protected by the building!"

"And the birds?" asked Jule staring hard at the trees.

"Lowering the nano walls now," said Helga

Salty winds gusted into the room, shaking the leaves of the trees that kept moving after the winds stilled.

"They made it! How do we lure them in here with us?" said Aria, looking for a ladder or something to bridge over to the trees.

"I have a plan." Nikau took out his phone and after a few swipes, his phone connected to the building audio system, emitting a cacophony of parrot calls.

"I've been studying kea language, and other species as well. I'm not sure who all is in the trees, so I made a program to cycle through the species in Adelaide."

"What are you telling them?" asked Aria, amazed.

"Roughly? Friends. Food. Safety. Peace."

Just then colors and shapes began to emerge from the trees, but none of the birds made the move to join them.

"They better hurry. The other wall of the eye is coming up quick," said Baraka looking into the distance.

A swirl of dark from the farthest tree headed for them. They took a step back, suspecting a small tornado had spun off from the typhoon.

"Black cockatoos! Yellow-tails and glossys! They must have blown in from Kangaroo Island, or got caught on the way inland,"

Jule said, nearly jumping with delight to see so many in one place.

After circling the trees, the birds swept into the room, crashing into the one nano inner wall Helga had left up.

"Here come the white cockatoos!" said Aria

"And the rosellas and lorikeets! And red-rumps, too," said Jule now spinning to see all the birds.

"This is more cockatiels than I've seen in my life!" gasped Aria.

"It's not just parrots. All kinds of species are mixed in with them," said Baraka.

A blast of wind shook the trees, shredding leaves into the air. Some parrots perched in the open storm room nearly blew out.

"We have to shut the walls," urged Helga.

"Wait, look, those aren't leaves. They're budgies! Hundreds of them!" said Aria. Tears streamed down her face. She reached out to Nikau and Jule to steady herself in the rising wind.

The budgies swirled into the room, circling overhead, wing to wing. As if on command, they dropped to the floor, carpeting every available space with green.

"Lower the walls!" yelled Nikau over the wind.

The room flipped to dark, except for thousands of soft-colored, silhouetted forms discovering that they could hang from the lowered inner nano-walls, preferring a higher perch where possible. The budgies didn't seem to mind the floor.

"Oh my god, it's like the Conference of the Birds!" said Baraka and recited from the book by the Sufi, Farid Attar.

"The home we seek is in eternity;
The Truth we seek is like a shoreless sea,
Of which your paradise is but a drop.

This ocean can be yours; why should you stop
Beguiled by dreams of evanescent dew?
The secrets of the sun are yours, but you
Content yourself with motes trapped in its beams.
Turn to what truly lives, reject what seems –
Which matters more, the body or the soul?
Be whole: desire and journey to the Whole."

The birds had grown quiet as had the humans, listening to Baraka, along with the outer storm and the silky shifting of feathers. The humans didn't speak or move, projecting calm for the winged wildness that had voluntarily sought sanctuary with them.

As the hours passed, an inner calmness settled on them all, none able to escape the obvious tragedy and beauty all around them.

Chapter 24
South Australia

Through the long hours, Nikau, like the birds, remained perched in the crowded corner, monitoring the weather measurements. The others, who had only had eyes for the birds, noticed when Nikau turned toward them. He broke the long silence. "The pressure has risen, and the winds are dying down. I think we can let them go."

Heads nodded in silent affirmation, and tears fell. The rising outer storm walls stirred the birds and one by one the nano-walls disappeared, freeing clouds of beauty into the grey skies, their cries sounding so much like joy that the humans shouted and danced.

"We are finally free from the laboratory walls," said Nikau as he joined Aria who was leaning as if she would take off and fly with the birds if she could.

"And we're on a beach at last. It came to us!" Aria smiled, wiping her face.

The parrots faded from sight.

The humans' eyes refocused from the far horizon to their surroundings, and there wasn't much they recognized. Where there had been cars on city streets, there were now boats checking the area for survivors and people to rescue.

"Hey, I've got a satellite signal," said Helga.

"Looks like they boosted the 6G network to reach us," said Tiago.

Their watches and phones dinged all at once, a chorus drawing them back from their magical trance.

"We can get back to work," said Helga, with regret in her voice.

Six heads bowed as if in prayer as they dug into their messages and the news reports.

"Oh great, Diwa wobbled over Adelaide and then went back out to sea. It's not heading to New Zealand, but in the opposite direction," said Aria, clearly relieved.

Jule said, "And the mob backed down at PACT! Our messages about prion transmission got out in time and not a single bird was harmed."

"But what about the cockatoo with the human eye? And we heard gunfire! I can't believe the RedDeaders wouldn't have kept shooting once they started. How can one press release stop a mob's momentum?"

Scrolling more, Jule said, "Ah, it says here that PACT found a video of – oh no, Ronnie's dead, Helga!"

"What happened?" said Helga taking a step back, bumping into Baraka who held out his hands to steady her.

"He died of PPDS or a heart attack or both. I'm so sad about this." Jule breathed deeply and promised herself she could cry later, not now. It's not what Ronnie would want. "PACT put together a video of Ronnie's last minutes, and holo-projected it all over the grounds. You remember what a great education and entertainment system they had to show what the forests used to look like and the birds that used to live there, including millions of passenger pigeons? They ran that, as well as Ronnie being comforted by the crazy cockatoos as he lay dying. He asked Hercules to take his eye and let the birds go. Do you remember Hercules?"

"I do, smart bird and devoted to Ronnie. But he always scared me a little bit," said Helga.

"I think the Reddeaders were scared of him, too, and also of all the witnesses. For every Reddeader there was someone from USSA and another from the Social Police. But after the holovideo, it says even some Reddeaders cried," said Jule.

"But what was the gunfire we heard?"

"Ha! They say it was the African greys mimicking gunfire!" said Nikau who linked into the report. "The news commentators say the mob devolved into an impromptu party, like a modern-day Woodstock. People are still arriving to see the Carolina parakeets flying free."

Jule projected her screen so that everyone could see the Carolina parakeets, nearly hunted twice to extinction, flying to the outdoor, raised platform feeders that had been quickly built around the sanctuary, birds and humans alike feasting.

"It looks like they had a Carolina parakeet release a little sooner than anticipated," said Helga smiling, but then she frowned at what cost it had come.

"I've got a message from Daku," said Aria. He says not to go downstairs because of heavy flooding and damage. He says there's a fire escape hidden in the wall that we can use."

"But where will we go?" asked Nikau, looking to Aria.

"Home," said Aria. "I want to go home."

"Okay, but we need to get out of this building first, and we aren't going anywhere with the water so high. We need a boat," said Jule.

"What if we left on that boat?" asked Tiago pointing to a sailboat tacking to them. "É *uma beleza*! And an ocean-class boat as well."

"Ahoy, mates," said the lone person aboard the boat. "Need a ride?"

"How about to New Zealand?" asked Aria.

"Well, funny you should ask. That's just where I was headed before the storm came up. She's all stocked and ready to go."

"You gotta be kidding me!" said Nikau. "Now we're in a happily-ever-after adventure."

"Not quite, I can't sail her myself. My crew is scattered to the winds, ha, literally."

"I can sail," said Tiago. "I've got a boat back in Brazil."

"Wait. You're willing to take me home?" Aria said.

Tiago said, "I can't think of anything I'd rather do. The lab is destroyed, the airport is demolished, and who knows how long the quarantine will last."

"Thanks," Aria said and squeezed his hand.

"Yes, this could work. With Luther's connections and the emergency situation, we can probably get our passports electronically validated. We are essential personnel, so they'd be glad for us to continue our work at your lab in Christchurch," said Jule.

"What, you're coming too?" Aria asked, her eyes tearing.

"Aria, I'm not going to leave you. Not now. Maybe not ever," Jule said embracing her.

Nikau joined them. "Ditto."

Baraka and Helga hung tentatively back, but the bond of

work and the storm pulled them hard in a direction even a few hours earlier they couldn't have imagined. The world was different, more alive, after holding inextricably intertwined beauty and tragedy.

The captain said, "Hate to break up the hug huddle, but I'm going to need more help than, what's your name? Tiago? It's a big boat and the seas are up."

"I know how to sail, too. And I've always wanted to see New Zealand. May I join you?" asked Baraka.

Jule's and Tiago's smiles were so large that the often-formal Baraka momentarily put his arms around their shoulders. All eyes turned to Helga, who was shaking her head. "I'm too old for such an adventure."

"But, Helga, we need you. There is so much research waiting to be done, and it can all happen in New Zealand. With your ethics, wisdom, and experience, you could guide us in restoring our relationship with the keas and the land," said Jule.

"Yes," said Aria, "the keas left us after one was shot. We need to rebuild their trust. There's been efforts to have keas awarded rights, like we did for our rivers. Maybe they need to be their own nation, like in Honduras."

"This could be doable, since we can communicate with them so much more easily these days," said Nikau.

"Everyone can stay at Kowhai Ranch. There's plenty of room. It's set up for volunteers and research. We can have that parrot pajama party that we never got to," said Aria with a glance at Jule and Nikau.

"I don't see how we can break up the team now," pleaded Jule. They all nodded in agreement, even the captain whose name they still hadn't asked.

"Alright, enough," said Helga. "You had me at 'we need you.' Besides, that Luther is an interesting fellow."

"Captain, what's your name?" asked Aria.

"Ted Smith. And my boat is Alice."

"You're not a serial killer, are you?" asked Nikau. "We don't want to enter a horror seascape film."

He tied off Alice to the emerged fire escape and waved his phone. "There, you've got my accreditations and letters of reference. I'm the best you can get."

Tiago studied the documents.

Aria said, "I'm calling Mom to tell her we have guests coming. Hey, Mom! I have you on speaker phone."

"Oh, Aria, I was so worried about you! *Como esta, mi hija?*"

"I'm super *bien*, Mama," Aria said as an upwelling sense of dependence washed over her until she realized it wasn't dependence, but interdependence. "Can I come home?"

"That's the second time I've been asked that in 24 hours. Isaac's here."

"Wow. That's great! Did he also ask if he could bring five friends with him? The parrot gang is coming with me."

"I can see we have a lot to talk about. When will you get here?"

"Let me ask. Captain, how long is the trip?"

Ted shrugged and said, "Seven to ten."

Aria said into the phone. "Seven to ten days. We'll talk more soon. I love you!"

"Oh, before you go, your cousin Kendi called."

"How is she?"

"For now, everything has worked out amazingly well. My homeland is the first nation to sign a peace accord with wildlife of any kind, and in this case, with the parrots of La Moskitia. Kendi thinks the macaws are calling themselves the **Guara**dians, a nation unto their own."

"Maybe New Zealand will be the second, and we can start with Kowhai Ranch."

"*Me gusta! Te almo.* Kia ora."

"Kia ora."

"No time like the present, shall we?" asked Ted, reaching for Aria's hand to welcome her aboard.

"Yes, let's get on it. Or should we stay here and help clean up and rescue people?" Aria said looking around at the destruction.

"I think we're needed more in New Zealand for research, and we can continue our work on the boat. The storm may be gone, but the disease emergency hasn't abated," said Helga.

"Oh, we have to work? I thought we were just going to sail off into the sunset and live happily ever after," said Nikau.

"That's a great idea, except we're heading east," said Aria.

"All right then, sailing into the morning's new light," said Nikau, sighting a ray of sun breaking through the moving clouds. He followed Aria to the front of the boat, where the sun shone through the rising sails.

"Having saved the human and parrot races, we have come to the perfect ending," said Aria, despite not knowing how much of a future she had. But she did know that this moment couldn't be better.

Nikau said, "It's not quite so perfect. Want to hear an update on the parrot neurological project Baraka, Tiago, and I didn't get to explain before the storm?"

"You said parrot brains don't show disease."

"They don't, but their brains are changing. We compared kea brain size and weights and they are getting bigger and more efficient."

"How?"

"Our hypothesis is that the prion is interacting with the LRRC37 gene analog in parrots."

"Okay, Brainiac, what's the LRRC37 gene?"

"It's a leucine-rich repeating/containing protein variant that parrots apparently obtained through convergent evolution. Their LRRCs don't have the same structure as those in humans, but they have similar functions."

"Which are?"

"They help protect brain tissue from degeneration and promote neural growth. It's hypothesized that parrots and people are so smart because of these gene paralogs. Even without these paralogs, studies have shown for years how other animals, especially those in close contact with humans, are also getting smarter. They have to be to navigate the increasing urban environments."

"Okay, so why is this bad news? I think it would be pretty cool to have even smarter parrots on the planet."

"Because we had Carol look at humans. It seems human children are developing marginally statistically less efficient brains, and the global II has been dropping."

"I thought that previous studies showed that lowering intelligence was a temporary response due to global stressors caused by the recent pandemics and climate change."

"That's part of it, but the PrK may also interact with the similar human LRRC gene and turn it off. It will probably have the most impact on the youngest."

"So, you're saying that children will be less smart if exposed to the PrK, which is everywhere!"

Nikau nodded in affirmation, wanting to hear the scientist in her work it out, especially since he hadn't yet. Aria looked into the horizon as she used her fingers to track her thinking.

"One, prions are really hard to destroy. It usually takes the most extreme temperatures to destroy them. Two, we know that in some soils exposed to weathering cycles of rain and drying, the prions can degrade over time. Three, exposing them to microbes and enzymes can neutralize them, but doing that over large patches of land is a daunting task." She lowered her hands and exhaled deeply. "So, we might be stuck with prions for several generations at least, but maybe in the not too far future things can return to normal, and the science, with our help, will catch up and fix this novel disease."

Taking her hand, Nikau said, "But free flying parrots will keep contaminating the land."

"Yes, we might not contract the neurological disease if we don't have parrots in captivity where we can get bitten, and because the digestive process might somehow cause the environmental prion proteins to misfold in a different way, but ingestion will cause the PrK to be present in children's bodies, resulting in decreased intelligence. But I'm guessing we'll find a way to block the process of prions turning off the LRRC gene."

"I hate to keep harping on the good news/bad news meme, but it's possible that the LRCC gene deactivation could be inherited. If it's turned off in one generation, that trait is passed on to the next generation."

"We didn't want children anyway, did we?" she asked turning from the ocean view to look into Nikau's eyes.

"Maybe not, especially now," he said taking her in his arms. "I don't know what the future, our work, and our vows will bring. But I know that whatever we give birth to will be beautiful."

Epilogue
Unknown location: sometime in the very far future

Bitner poked her head out of her reed-woven tent at first light. The cavern was finally quiet after a disturbing night. She'd fallen asleep only a few hours ago. The cyclone-force winds pounded the wood door that rattled the iron hinges so loud she couldn't hear herself think. She and others had cried out every time one of the conelaten evergreen trees' crowns was sheared from the trunk, or one of the many other tree species splintered at the base and crashed to the ground. Her field was archeology, but she knew the names of all the trees, as did everyone in her chosen klatch. Throughout the night she worried that the heavy trees would break through the cavern roof that shuddered with each impact. The cavern's floors seemed alive with the waves of vibrations of falling trees. Echoes of the impact bounced from the shuddering cavern roof to the increasing puddles that vibrated as if a mammoth had just trod past. She reasoned that the floor had hummed and seemed to roll at times because the shocks of the trees falling had set off some kind of harmonics with the cavern structure, or maybe she drank too much ipu last night.

If it had been that bad inside, she dreaded seeing the destruction outside. The winds had mostly died down hours earlier.

The camp had no light source aside from the oil pottery bowls, and she'd been afraid to venture out on her own before now. She wasn't moving quickly, and felt tired and groggy. No one in the excavating camp had slept much because the cyclone party had gone on late, because the fierce winds had threatened to destroy their camp, and because of possible flooding that would seep through the cavern walls that enclosed their lean-tos, tents, and sleeping pads. She was grateful they'd been below ground and spared an immense beating above ground. If her parents had known how scared she'd be or that the towering trees would be shorn in two, they would never have let her go. They'd been skeptical about her dabbling in this new, unproven field of archeology. Bitner decided not to say anything, about last night to her parents. Besides maybe she wouldn't ever want to be out in the wilderness again if it meant another night like that.

Glad that the door hadn't been sealed shut by the fallen trees, she climbed over enormous trunks and newly fallen rock scree to see the muddy bay. Its waves normally lapped the forest edge near her camp. At first, she thought the damage amounted to only heavy clean-up to clear the path to the bay and their main excavation site.

At the top of the path, she said, "What!" at the destruction below. The bay had disappeared! She thought there must have been an earthquake that was muted by the howling winds and thundering tree falls. She may have had too much ipu, but her body was on full alert, the revelry of the night before and its consequences disappearing.

The sacred mother rust tree, once by the shore, now teetered on the edge of a new crumbling cliff about to plunge into the mud flats. Before she could stop herself, both feet jumped to the ledge below, frantic to stop the tree's fall. There weren't many trees like these giant rust trees that grew along the coast, but the thinking was that there had once been many more. Archaeology excavations had yielded petrified wood of many of this tree's ancestors. The tree was one reason she'd chosen this summer internship, and, another reason, was to see the ocean every day. Also, some of the petrified fragments had shown evidence of burning. It was possible that her ancient ancestors had lived along these shores. She longed to know the story of her people's journey. Scientists suspected that her kind didn't suddenly appear in the biotic community, the only advanced species on the planet, but had slowly evolved like all the other species, maybe even from other species. But they hadn't found irrefutable proof, neither fossils nor archeological evidence. She had hoped that would change during her summer at this once promising site. But now it was destroyed. Their excavation pits were flooded with mud or had disappeared with the bay, and the rust mother tree threatened to bury what remained under a layer of splintering divinity.

She ran to the overhanging tree and walked up its exposed, massive roots. The roots were nearly as immense as the trunk and reached deep down and far out from the trunk base. She hadn't realized she was softly keening until she stopped when her eyes caught on something sticking out half-way up the cliff. It was something embedded in the crumbling sandstone of the newly exposed cliff. She quickly climbed up to the object.

The object bore straight and slightly curved lines that didn't resemble anything she'd seen before, though she'd been trained to imagine artifacts as if they were three dimensional before being squeezed flat through the geological processes that had preserved them. Enclosed in the mesh of the curving lines was something more, a dark shadow that was different, a fossil! She knew it wasn't good technique, but she was desperate and pulled on the sandstone and mud conglomeration. As she dislodged it, as if she'd pulled a plug from a dike, the cliff began to melt in front of her. A deafening crack jolted her as the tree trunk fractured and fell toward her. She flew down the cliff's slush, riding on a sandstone slab. She screamed as she dodged falling debris that thundered past her. The exploding tree branches blasted her even farther and faster until she lost her balance and ended up face-first in the mud that had been the ancient bay's bottom.

"Bitner! Are you okay?" Finlu called, rushing to her, followed by others from the camp.

This isn't how Bitner wanted Finlu or anyone to find her, spitting mud as she stood up. She did have enough sense to be grateful that they'd found her.

"You almost didn't make it! What were you doing up on the cliff face?" he asked.

She pointed to the artifact that she'd risked her life for. "I wanted to be close to Mother Rust to see if I could help her. Then I found this. It was buried in her roots."

The others stepped closer. They looked like their spirits were jumping out of their skulls. The fossil enmeshed in the curved and straight lines had feathers and a large hooked beak, like a parrot. She felt what they felt, and they keened together until the lead professor called, "What's the matter? Get away from that cliff face."

The wisdom in her words was obvious, but they were loath to leave the object, and loathe to touch it. Bitner said to Finlu, "Mother Rust gave up her life to bring this to us. I can't refuse what she's asked us to protect, as much as I want to. Will you help me?"

"I'll help you take this to Dr. Kemli." Finlu strutted forward, maybe too proud that he was often the first to respond to a request, which, according to custom, each who heard a request was obliged to accept.

As they bent to hoist the object, the other young ones helped. They climbed up the path to camp, softly murmuring to one another as they lifted the object over trunks, rocks, and newly formed muddy hillocks. Dr. Kemli was warming herself by the campfire, chewing her morning kafe beans. "Well, that certainly was a night. First off, Bitner, are you okay?"

"Yes, Doctor."

"Everyone else?" she asked, giving each a close look. "Good. Now, what in burning-trunk were you thinking?"

Bitner thought she must be angry because she'd never heard her swear before.

"First wandering away from camp alone," she said, eyeing Bitner severely, "and then taking samples without studying them properly in place. Please tell us your story."

"Mother Rust seemed to be in trouble, and the cliff side was unstable, so I felt like I had to take this before we lost it."

"And?"

"And when I saw it, I was astounded and had to study it further."

"Well, that's the sign of a good archeologist, curiosity and drive. Looking at the cliff, I can see you came out on top of the situation. But next time it could kill you, and you might destroy our only chance to understand the past. Let's see what you have."

Bitner had been standing in front of the object, as if she could hide her shame, but moved away. Dr. Kemli took a closer look.

"Oh my, this is remarkable. So far, we can't see how old this fossil is. We will have to work on the cliff, safely, to see where this particular fossil belongs on the geologic timeline. It could be quite old, although the seismic changes in this area, as we experienced last night, could have rapidly buried objects from the past, and fossils can form quite quickly. These curved and straight lines could be plant material, but of something built, not grown. Possibly it's wood since metal rarely fossilizes, but we can't rule it out. Now as to the species of fossil surrounded by the lines? Hmm. See the hip articulation here? Clearly this marks this species as one of the most ancient group of known vertebrate species, a particular kind of reptile. They evolved into birds, lost their teeth, and their arms evolved to wings, such as in this fossil. So, we know we have a bird, and the hooked beak suggests a parrot. But the cranium looks different, not as large as modern parrots, but I can't be sure. This could be the missing link we've been looking for. Did you see any other artifacts near it? Any other fossils?"

"No, just this. I didn't have time to do anything but grab it as I fell."

"The cliff could have dislodged more hidden treasures, as could have the empty bay. There is no time to waste. The water might return, and the cliff face may break apart even more, burying what has been exposed. Let's divide into two teams, one to clean up camp and the other to do a quick survey."

Nobody moved. They stared at the fossil, the first of its kind. Dr. Kemli looked up into the faces of the crew and saw their silence wasn't just the shock of the storm and the loss of Mother Rust that froze them. It was what surrounded the fossil.

"What's this?" asked Bitner pointing to the lines around the fossil.

"It could be what was called a cage in ancient stories."

"But those stories were made up to entertain us, or scare us into right action."

"All myths have a kernel of the truth. Let me tell you of our journey."

The professor knew she would need to help the team absorb the significance of the discovery. As was custom, they responded, "We will hear of our journey," and settled down to listen and learn, still anxious but comforted by the familiar routine.

"In the middle of life's journey on the land, lived the Last People. They didn't know freedom, so locked were they in an ancient war of survival, fear, and desire. They caged everything they touched, even their own minds and hearts. As they multiplied, so grand were their villages and refuse dumps that they imprisoned Earth, which withered under their killing embrace.

They were doing what they had evolved to do, their journey's path set. They were hunters and eaters of flesh, killers of their own kind and kin, racing to their own demise. They stole others from their own paths to become captives on the path of the more powerful.

In the last days, the Last People formed an army of destruction, pillaging everything and everyone in their path, until they could go no farther, for they had arrived at a towering cliff that stretched beyond sight inland and into the sea. They couldn't go around it, and if they tried to climb it, the cliff's dangerous slopes would kill them. No one could see what lay on top of the cliff or the dangers they would encounter if they climbed. The end of their journey story could not be divined. The army stalled, unable to decide their course. Some suggested they go back the way they came, even though it was wasteland. Many returned anyway. Others could choose to return to the sea and devolve before the time of telling of stories. Many disappeared into the sea, and their stories were lost for all time.

One of the later born had a dream that people released their captives, and their hearts became lighter, seeing others rejoice in freedom. In the dream, people let go of their possessions and control, and they lightened even more, not carrying the burden of false assurance. In the dream, with their limbs free of what they had grasped so carelessly, they were able to hold one another and together soar in spirit.

Upon the telling of the dream the next day, the army released their captives, possessions, and control, and embraced each other into their hearts. And they soared up and over the cliff, learning that none can fly free until all fly free. And so, the Last became the First."

"Are you saying this really happened?" asked one.

"Do we come from the Last or the First People?" asked Finlu.

"Were we the caged or the captors?" asked Bitner

"Yes," answered the professor.

Bitner thought it wouldn't be a journey story if it didn't include paradox. But the object she'd found was real. "But what about this?" She pointed to the fossil and cage.

"I would hear your thoughts."

Turning it over, she said, "It could be part of a religious custom of burying the dead, perhaps with the cage door open signaling an understanding of freedom in death and in life?"

"Perhaps you're projecting our own understandings onto the past?"

"Or it could be from a time when parrots were captive, and the stories are more than myth and religion," said Finlu.

"Which we won't know until we search and research," said the professor.

"I'm afraid," said Bitner, "of what's in that cliff. Of who we once were. Of who we could become again. The cliff almost killed me."

The others listened as she puzzled out her journey, a story in the making.

Bitner continued, "But to not take up the quest is to turn our backs on knowledge and the future. We risk going back to where we came." She didn't say she felt a bond with the Last People. She couldn't explain this new feeling, but somehow, deep within her, was the destroyer of trees, and the eater and captor of others. Oddly, that realization was a relief. She thought that knowing the story of her people, she could choose, she could know herself. She whispered, "I am the first and the last." The truth broke through her subconscious, a sudden clarity felling her self-concept as if it were a tree and she tumbled to the ground.

"You don't journey alone," said Finlu, who helped her stand.

"We'll explore the cliff and empty bay together," said the professor.

Bitner felt lighter. Like the Last People, she had been grasping, carrying an unnecessary burden, and certainly not alone.

"Fly free with me!" she called as she ran along a path that rose behind the camp.

Unable to refuse, first Finlu, then the other interns and finally Dr. Kemli followed her up the slope of the mountain to the Landing well above the cliff's edge. It was a rocky outcrop where they often came to take in the wide view of the mountains that gradually slipped into the bay, except now there was a sharp scar formed by the crumbling cliff. They looked around at each other and cried, "Fly free!"

Bitner jumped, and then the others. They fell toward the empty bay until their wings caught the uprising wind. Bitner flew over the empty bay, then turned back toward the cliff and thunder clouds. A beam of light broke through the retreating storm clouds, highlighting the winged beauty of the others below her. Circling, she saw how life's journey is like a circle. There is both a looking back and a looking forward along the way. The wind that alternatively ruffled and sleeked her feathers tight to her face offered her this ancient wisdom and new promise:

If you look back to face the future
And if you look inward to face the past
You will be able to look outward
and see your face in all others.
Bind yourself not to desire
But kiss joy as it flies free.

Context to Reality

Status of Wild Parrots – Parrots are the most endangered group of birds in the world, with over 50% of the species declining in populations and 25% endangered. The causes for this are mainly the wildlife trade and trafficking (legal and illegal), as well as habitat loss. The official last Carolina parakeet, Inca, a native parrot of North America, died at the Cincinnati Zoo in 1918, although probable sightings occurred later than that in the Southeastern USA. The keas' numbers are decreasing on the South Island of New Zealand. There are less than 2,000 wild sun parakeets left in the world. Moas and the northern Kaka (related to Keas) have gone extinct since humans inhabited the island. The great green macaw of the Americas is endangered, with approximately 70 left in Honduras.

Parrot Captivity – There are hundreds of millions of parrots in captivity on every continent but Antarctica, most of which cannot fly, and they live in diminished circumstances. Trafficked parrots are still trapped from the wild, legally and illegally, and their suffering and death rates are high. Parrots are wild animals who often do not make good pets for many reasons, such as parrots who can become aggressive as they age. Humans often give them up to sanctuaries, which are beyond capacity in the USA.

<u>Parrot Diseases</u> – There are no prion diseases in parrots or any avian prion diseases transmissible to humans. Prions do exist in parrots, as does the LRRC gene analog that contributes to their intelligence, one of the highest of all animals. Parrots have many viruses and other disease agents that they are at risk from and are a risk to other parrot and avian populations. Some of these diseases are transmissible to humans. The movement of parrots around the world has led to the spread of these diseases, which are generally low risk for humans. However, they remain a threat to wild parrot populations, especially those stressed and existing in low numbers in fragmented ecosystems, which, unfortunately, is the majority of parrots.

<u>Parrot Conservation and Liberation</u> – The spix macaw is extinct in the wild, and birds have been moved from various collections in Europe to Brazil where they are awaiting release. Scientists are considering de-extinguishing the Carolina parakeet (that is, using scientific methods of genetic manipulation to bring an extinct species back into existence). Rosa's story is a true one, and she died in 2016 in La Moskitia, Honduras, having been rescued by the Miskitu parrot conservation project, Apu Pauni. This project of indigenous people protects the last stand of naturally distributed scarlet macaws in Honduras, decreasing nearly 100% poaching of nests in 2014 to less than 10% by 2020. Captive parrots should not be released into the wild without protocols that ensure birds' safety and freedom from disease. The health and well-being of parrots, forests, and people are inextricably interrelated. Parrots as seed dispersers are important for biodiversity health. If the people who live in communities where parrots are naturally found are not flourishing, in terms of spiritual, physical, economic, and social

health, it's probable that the parrots aren't either. Conservation oriented toward community health and well-being is paramount when considering the prospects for sustainable and viable parrot populations

<u>Prion Disease in Humans.</u> These are caused by misfolded brain prion proteins that cause misfolding in other prion proteins. These then attach to brain tissue and cause damage. Humans acquire the disease through genetic disorders and ingestion, or from blood exposure to contaminated tissue in affected animals. To date, they result in 100% fatality. Several treatments are being investigated at this time.

Besides Rosa, all other characters are fictional and do not represent any living person or parrot.

Acknowledgements

I give thanks to the first reader of this book, Gail Koelln, who gave me the encouragement to seek other readers and publication. Gail also led as the graphic designer for the cover and lead publisher at One Earth Conservation Publishing. Pat Latas is my colleague in all things parrot and was the second reader and incredible artist who gave us the cover art. A huge bow of gratitude to Jane Edwards, not only for her gift of editing this book through several rewrites, but for encouraging me to write many years ago. With her heart and wisdom, she brings the same out of my words. Thank you to Charlotte Patterson, whose eye for clarity and beauty reviewed the manuscript, correcting and encouraging, and to Patricia Guianne who gave of her time and skill to edit the book. Kari Schmidt was my go-to avian geneticist for working out how to write about de-extinction, not just using science but heart and ethics. For good company and the finer points on Carolina parakeets, I thank Kevin Burgio.

There were many others, avian and non, whose precious life experiences and courage inspired this story. I thank them for the hope that they give not just to me, but perhaps also to each reader, to whom I am grateful for sharing with me this tale. May you have found more connection, amazement and courage in your life, for the sake of all life.

Connecting to One Earth Conservation's Work and Vision as Portrayed in Prion

This novel is published by One Earth Conservation (One Earth) as a means to serve parrots and people everywhere. You can find out more about the book, access discussion questions, and purchase associated merchandise by visiting our website.

One Earth is a U.S.-based 501(c)(3) not-for-profit organization that seeks to heal human systems that diminish individual worth and separates humans artificially from the rest of nature in many ways. We affirm that people must be healthy and develop multiple intelligences so all of life, individuals, and human and biotic systems on Earth can flourish. One Earth's mission is building knowledge, motivation, resilience, and capacity in people, organizations, and communities in the United States and internationally so that they can better cherish and nurture themselves, nature, and other beings. This is achieved by combining work directed outward toward other beings (our conservation work with parrots in the Americas) and outward towards nature with work directed inward toward one's own human nature (our Nurture Nature Program), as outer well-being and inner well-being are inseparable and mutually beneficial. One Earth invites people into a vision and transformational practice of *interbeing*, based on:

1. All individuals of all species have inherent worth and dignity (all bodies are beautiful, have worth, and matter).
2. All individuals of all species are connected to each other

in worth, beauty and well-being.

3. We are also connected in harm. There is no beauty without tragedy. What is done to another, is done to all of us.

4. Embracing this reality, humans grow in belonging to this wondrous planet and the life upon it, and so embraced and nurtured, can nurture in return.

5. This reality of interbeing makes us both powerful and vulnerable, therefore, we need each other to grow and to heal as much as possible.

6. Humans are adaptable and can change, both individually and as families, organizations, communities, and societies. We can become more effective and joyful nurturers and "naturers." This is hard, deep, intentional, and a lifetime's work.

To join our team, you can sign up for our e-newsletter, where we report on our work in the world with endangered parrots in the Americas and list upcoming events and activities. We also enjoy working with volunteers who seek to serve life through One Earth, such as by helping with organizational growth, social media, and conservation. You may also join our Parrot Conservation Corps, a year-long program focused on parrots, but adaptable to working with wildlife, social justice, and conservation anywhere.

For more information, visit www.oneearthconservation.org

About the Author

LoraKim combines her experience as a wildlife veterinarian, Unitarian Universalist minister, and Certified Trainer in Nonviolent Communication to address the importance of both human and nonhuman well-being in living a deeply meaningful and vibrant life, as well as caring for self, family, relationships, organizations, and life all around. She serves as a Community Minister affiliated with the Community Unitarian Universalist Congregation at White Plains, NY, and Co-director of One Earth Conservation. She is an inspiring speaker and leads nation-wide workshops and webinars in Compassionate Communication and Nurturing Nature. With over 33 years of experience working with parrot conservation in the Americas, she currently leads projects in Guatemala, Honduras, Nicaragua, Guyana, and Paraguay, and is developing projects in Suriname, French Guiana, Brazil, and El Salvador. You can read about her life and work in her memoir, "Conservation in Time of War." With Gail Koelln, Co-director of One Earth Conservation, she has authored, "Nurturing Discussions and Practices."

Other Books by LoraKim Joyner

Conservation in Time of War: A Transformational Journey through Beauty and Tragedy

Nurturing Discussion: Nurturing Nature, Yourself, and Your Relationships (with co-author Gail Koelln)

Published by One Earth Conservation

Made in United States
North Haven, CT
18 July 2023

39139832R10168